BEING EATEN BY A CROCODILE

In our sex lives we live underground
and are at war with the world
Robert Lindner

BEING EATEN BY A CROCODILE

a novel

by

COLIN HUGGETT

First published 2023

ISBN 978-1-913144-46-3

PENNILESS PRESS PUBLICATIONS
Website :www.pennilesspress. co. uk/books

CHAPTER 1

To look at, there was nothing about the man driving home alone from an evening class to indicate or suggest he was about to commit a murder. In fact, he wasn't to know it himself, and even when it had taken place continued to find himself still trying to come to terms with how and why it had happened so suddenly like that.

Dark-haired, in his late twenties, on the thin side, there was a natural pensiveness about his fairly boyish good looks that told you little more than the concentration being given to his driving on the rain-filled road that night, along with the previous two to three hours spent trying to juggle with the intransigence of French verbs and how with each passing session having a better understanding of them seemed to get further and further away. He had considered giving them up, the class, that is, as there seemed no real point in submitting oneself to such hopeless, unnecessary torture when all you needed to know once in France is the few everyday sentences you knew off by heart, and then open the ubiquitous phrase book when in difficulty. In some ways it was more fun like that. But even as his mind passed over these lines of retreat, they also brought into play the sights and sounds, food and drink, of the country itself, when in a matter of months he and his wife Anna would be immersing themselves in that warm sun and hypnotic summer blue of its sea and sky.

It was just after nine o'clock; tired, he hadn't been sleeping too well, yet it wasn't so much tiredness coupled with the effort to conjugate another language that stole over him as he had driven out of the college parking area, as a deeper, oddly-centred dispiritedness at again nearing the end of another day in which barely nothing of any real substance had happened to lighten the familiar routine that now brought its fatigue to him like a

1

deadening weight, and which in the many intrinsic ways it manifested itself was another reason why he has so impulsively signed up for the evening class some weeks before.

The rain adding its dreary greyness to the monotonous swishing of the windscreen wipers, joined neon lights bouncing off the surface of the road on this wet November night in a conspiracy highlighting not only the dark loneliness of the fields flashing past but also that other inner longing that went on searching for something different and more stimulating than doing the same things day after day. And so it was, that at a singular moment when he changed gear and left the roundabout behind, that fate and coincidence, intervening as they so often did to change everything forever, stepped in to bring the car to a stop alongside the solitary, rain-swept figure waiting for a bus. This wasn't something that had been planned or premeditated with someone in mind, and it was only afterwards, his thoughts racing aimlessly ahead of him, that he then realised he'd never been that close to someone who is dead before, and so in a position to see just how rapidly the transition is from life to non-existence, and in that second, those first few apprehending moments, refused to believe it, didn't want to, and for a time sat staring at the abruptly-stilled body slumped awkwardly in the seat beside him, the flush that had been agitating her features in those last few minutes now quickly fading as that other pallor – pale and strange – come into the face and complexion. Momentarily he thought she could so easily have been sleeping, except that there was no sight or sound of breathing, and not so intent on dying and in taking with her that brief liberating madness that had brought the taste of one's own blood to the mouth not so long before. Perfect, *unapproachable*, hers had been the stark and poignant simplicity of an appeal epitomised by those magical words, youth, adolescence, and which now, despite his growing fears and apprehension, went on remaining part of a remembered enchantment he had once felt would never come to an end, and which in a forever changing world intent on taking it away he had come to know as the longest dream of all.

Now in her early-forties, Anna's fading good looks and rounding figure were more than compensated for by the cheerful thoughtfulness of someone desperately in love with Ted, her husband, a younger man to whom she was devoted in the motherly anxious way that came so naturally to her, when, following an earlier misplaced relationship and a divorce that was less than amicable, it was as though she had been gifted a second chance of happiness when she least expected it. There were, of course, hiccups and bumps in their marriage, it was far too naïve to expect anything less, as she had mistakenly done in her previous marriage. Ted was kind, if a little withdrawn and insecure, but she put this down to his background and innate sensitivity, and which sometimes showed itself in the habit he had of crying for no apparent reason, tears streaming down his cheeks as his mood switched from a sunny carefreeness to silent reticence, to, on other occasions, an outbreak of emotion and uncontrollable sadness that left him clinging to her like a child. Minutes later he would be himself again, making her laugh as he came out with outrageous, impromptu remarks or quotations gleaned from the books he spent hours lost in, as he got the tea ready when she came in from work, again letting her know how lucky she was despite any misgivings and misunderstandings that arose from time to time and which she was only too ready to forgive or overlook. Having learnt to be happy with what she had, she didn't unduly question his lateness in getting back from the evening class, for as she knew, they often finished later than usual, with Ted going for a coffee with some of the others when it ended.

In the kitchen, having put out the food she had prepared – being that late it was only a snack – she took it through to the

3

lounge, placing it on the small coffee table in front of the sofa where they mostly spent the evenings watching television or a film when Ted was there. Having done this and caught up on the early evening's news, in an attempt to calm her nerves she had taken to sitting at the window in anticipation of seeing the car draw up below, and it was this she had been doing when he finally arrived home at a time so much later than on any other occasion, rushing to meet him at the door and saying, "Thank God you're back!" giving him a relieved smile as she leaned forward to peck him on the cheek, hers reaching out to touch his hand or arm as she had a habit of doing. "I was starting to think you'd had an accident."

"No such luck," he replied, in the droll, quietly cynical manner she liked, and which made her smile again as he kissed her on the cheek in return before brushing past her to go to the bathroom. "Shan't be long, just having a quick shower," he called over his shoulder, shutting the door behind him.

"I hope you're hungry, I've made a snack for us," she said, the warm, thankful gratitude filling her as she turned to follow him along the corridor being compensation for her earlier fears and doubts. Overtaken by the coldly numbing fear invading every part of his being, he had just managed to reach the bathroom before retching up, as he had done on the way back when forced to stop in a lay-by and vomit into the grass verge through the opened door of the car, before falling back into the seat, his hands riveted to the steering wheel as he tried to regain the composure to drive on. Undressed in the shower, he was even more exposed and vulnerable, and had been wrong in thinking it would freshen him up as more waves of fear and nausea made him feel like being sick again. Shaking, and barely managing to dry and dress himself, the sight of Anna and the familiar surroundings he had tried to console himself with during the frightening drive back, became instead an unreality the moment

4

he stepped into the bright lights of the lounge to find himself in the safety of a world he knew was about to be taken from him. Unable to eat, to take anything more than a few hesitant mouthfuls of food, she asked him if he was okay, that he looked rather pale, and that he was perhaps coming down with something, but all he could do was say he was tired, that he'd feel better in the morning, but which, even as he was saying it and on the edge of falling into the blackest pit of all, he knew would be a lie.

CHAPTER 2

When Detective Chief-Inspector John Richards heard that a couple looking for autumn mushrooms had come across the body of a young girl, the picture of an isolated woodland with a naked or partly-clothed body hastily covered with leaves and bracken came immediately into his mind, as it had a habit of doing at such times when based on personal experience gained over a lifetime in the police force. Nearing retirement, a tall, broad-shouldered man with a fine head of greying hair above a friendly face, he knew that such crimes were invariably committed on the spur of the moment by someone trying to avoid arrest after a rape or some other form of violence usually of a sexual nature. After thirty-five years involving him in all kinds of murder, he had no illusions about what was to be found in this or any other beautiful woodland or forest, having, so to speak, been there, seen it, and come away far too many times with the sad misgivings that came to him now when he heard the body was that of a teenage girl. If there were to be crimes involving dead bodies, he would have preferred it to be those in which the victim was some villain or gangster (as the press had taken to calling them) they were well rid of, and the body to have been hidden in a hole someone had dug with a spade or shovel they had been considerate enough to bring along. It did mean the police having to go to all the trouble of digging them up when they were subsequently found, but at least they hadn't been left sprawled wantonly about to frighten members of the public out jogging or collecting blackberries or mushrooms, such as happened in this particular case it seemed. Over many years, he had yet to come across anyone responsible for this sort of murder to have been so premeditated in what they were about to do, that they had brought along a shovel or spade with this in mind, which, among other things, was one of the reasons why they were caught so soon.

Rape, with or without an implement of burial, sent a small shiver through him and he gave a mental grimace towards the interplay of words as they flickered involuntarily across his mind as he once again went on finding some difficulty in acceding to the idea that he had spent so much of his working life being concerned with murder and other mindless crimes, he had begun thinking like their perpetrators. This, then, was how he had come so swiftly to the conclusion that however upsetting, this was yet another of those instances in which paedophilia was increasingly involved and which he felt inclined to let one of his other, younger colleagues to deal with. At best, it would mean tramping about through wet and muddy conditions after heavy overnight rain, while waiting about for who knows how long as forensics did their job in collecting evidence related to time of death, footprints and car tyres, and any other finds to be associated with the crime. Then there were the inevitable records and databases to be checked, along with the Sex Offenders Register, and if all went well, as it so often did in these open and shut cases, the person responsible would be under lock and key in no time at all. Add to this brief summary the very deep dislike he had of seeing the bodies of young people violated in this way, and he had every good reason to let someone else handle an abhorrent situation, telling himself as he put down the phone informing him that a body had been found, that the only real difference between this crime and so many others like it, being that it had been found by someone our mushrooming and not as it usually was by someone walking their dog.

However, as this and a dozen other unrelated matters about the day ahead flashed through his mind and he was about to leave the office, his phone rang again, and picking it up and hearing more about the situation at the murder scene as fuller details came in, his latent interest was revived somewhat by the news that this was not a run of the mill sex attack, as the girl in question had not been raped or sexually assaulted, and neither had her clothing been removed or interfered with as far as could be ascertained by preliminary investigation. Not someone who could be accused of walking away from anything new or original, murder without an apparent motive meant that within minutes of hearing this he was in a car commandeered from the station car park and being driven through open countryside on the edge of the town by a constable he had latched onto on his way out of the building, his curiosity racing ahead of them as the word, "Why?" floated in and out of the equation carrying him along with it. Had *he*, or to be politically correct, in a somewhat daft way, *she*, been disturbed? Even as it came into his head he dismissed the idea of a female being involved for although violence among lesbians was common, murder itself was rare. Then again, if they had been disturbed this in itself was unlikely allowing for the time (night) and the place itself, off the beaten track from what he knew of it. Impotence? Loss of control before the act had taken place? He didn't think so, even as these conjectures bobbed up from among a whole flotilla of possibilities, rational or otherwise. With a robbery or mugging, you knew for certain what they were after, but with something like sex it was a minefield open to the zaniest guesswork when the obvious pieces failed to fit.

But spell it as you liked, paedophilia had no other motive or underlying reasons but sexual gratification, at least he had never chanced upon any before now, and the fact that this case was turning out to be beyond the general scheme of things, glowed like a fire waiting to be put out in his restlessly, enquiring brain. All the more surprising then, that over the next twenty-four hours, having been to the scene, spoken to the couple, heard what forensics had to say, and then waited in the hope of coming across some explanation or other as officers sifted through the minutiae of computerised data related to the ever-lengthening list of sex offenders and crimes committed, he was even more intrigued when one of the duty officers at the reception desk hurried into his office to tell him there was someone in a bit of a state waiting there who had declared himself to be the person they were looking for.

CHAPTER 3

At the flat, Anna was vainly trying not to be too upset at finding her husband wasn't there when she came in from work just after five o'clock. Prone to a worry not short of anxiety when routine was inexplicably altered, she had changed from her office clothes into the less formal ones she wore at home, before starting to prepare the evening meal, and then sat down to look through the morning's unopened post to see if there was anything apart from junk mail that needed seeing to. At the same time, as another thirty minutes and then an hour passed, she was aware of this and other pointless exercises as little more than futile outlets for her growing concern as she went on telling herself Ted had either lost track of time while at the library, or was perhaps in the park feeding the ducks and swans as he was in the habit of doing, even though it was dark by then. To confirm and assuage her anxiousness, she even checked the bread bin to see if the loaf that had been there that morning was still intact or only partly used, and seeing that half of it was missing, felt temporarily reassured and more relaxed, if still on edge, as she had been two nights before when he had been so late in coming home. But when he still wasn't back by 6.30, the ominous dark emptiness of the road had become an inexorable part of the flurry of questions she had no answers to, and which, as she rushed to answer the ringing of the telephone, were then turned into another kind of turmoil at hearing it wasn't Ted on the other end of the line but a police officer asking her to come down to the station.

As she was trying to pull herself together while getting ready to do this, Ted was sitting between Detective Chief-Inspector Richards and another officer called Williams in the rear of an unmarked police car travelling back from the wood where the body had been found. Now and then there was some weirdo or other only too happy to waste police time by putting their name to something they hadn't done, and taking Ted there was a necessary procedure to make sure he knew where the body had been and not someone wishing to claim attention and a brief notoriety for himself until the truth came out and it had been proved to belong to a fantasy. At the same time, the claims of this young man who said his name was Edward Green, or Ted as he liked to be called, seemed genuine enough, for how else would he have known about the place and the event itself so soon after it had happened and which even now had not as yet been divulged publicly. Besides which, if he wasn't responsible for the girl's death and only faking an involvement, he was a very good actor in showing all the signs of distress and remorse the officers were so familiar with on these occasions; one of the chief characteristics of the fantasist owning up to something they had never done was their matter-of-fact and often boastful attitude by which they credited themselves with even the most hideous act.

CHAPTER 4

Like so many others before him, and with, no doubt, an infinite number to follow in his footsteps, he had been clutching at straws in hoping that once the initial shock had faded, the nauseous dread would go away. But after a sleepless night in which reality and the deepening nightmare were ineradicably twisted, all that happened was for it to have fastened itself permanently inside him like some fearful, incurable sickness or fever whose delirium refused to shut out the constantly recurring images of the night before. He was fully aware of what he had done, but where among these repercussions plunging him into the throes of despair was the reason for it when he had liked being with her so much.

"Are you sure you'll be alright?" Anna had asked more than once, leaning across to kiss him as he sat at the kitchen table before she left for work. "I can always take the day off it you want."

"I'll be okay," he had replied, having trouble with the words jamming themselves in the back of his throat and the wall of ice cutting him off from everything around him. She had kissed him, but finding himself so remote from the kitchen and her touch, it was as if neither of them were really there. Racked with fear and loathing, and unable to shut his eyes for more than a few minutes at a time, he had got up in the night, but after he had disturbed Anna and telling her he was okay and that he was only going to the bathroom, they were already living in the two entirely conflicting worlds: she the one he had been part of not so long ago, and he this other, extreme one taking him further away from it in a relentless, downward spiral he could do nothing to halt as it went on reminding him of other, more enjoyable days he never would know again. And although long before he felt he had known the meaning of the phrase when coming across it in some book or other, it was only then he recognised its fullest significance: a living death.

Alone in the kitchen, the radio but an alien, incoherent droning in the background, he was being forced by an innate instinct for self-preservation, into aimlessly trying to focus on a horror which went on clutching at him but for which there was no real answer or solution. Instead of daylight and the sounds of the street coming alive in the pale November sunshine, he was remorselessly pulled back into unending wet emptiness of the night before as it went on remaining solidly indifferent to what he begged of it. Later still, unable to stay in the flat or indeed, anywhere his tormented state of mind would let him, and driving being out of the question – he could barely stop his hands from shaking – he tried to find some solace or relief in going for a walk, of going somewhere, only to find that the second he found himself on the pavement with the sight and noise of the traffic all around him, than the numbing sickness that had overtaken him when driving back from the wood, again moved quickly from his jellied legs into the stomach, neck and head, there to fix itself behind the eyes like some lethargic anchor dragging him down and down again into its disabling pitiless depths. Even when by some tortuous route he had literally managed to drag himself into the quieter spaces of the park and the sound of the traffic receded to a less insistent hum on its outskirts behind the trees, it would still not leave him completely alone and able to forget, let alone allow him to fully recall what his life had been like before confused foreboding changed memory and recollection into the gaping abyss into which he was being swallowed.

Was it only a day ago he had walked along that same path an entirely different person, even though at the time, in looking around for something new to focus on and dwelling briefly on the evening class to come, he was always aware of being someone to

13

whom things happened without ever being certain why. Hadn't it always been like that with him, never being happy or content like Anna, who seemed to think that life was agreeable and to be liked for itself, when at the best of times it all seemed pretty much the same to his way of thinking. While now, by comparison, and seen through the static prism of the unreality he was enmeshed in, he was seeing the past as being something he had only grazed before and failed to see for what it was. But *Julie* had been real, hadn't she, and not only what is called a figment or shadow of the imagination. They had met there by the lake, by chance, earlier in the summer, as even now, among the distortions and confrontations bearing down in their attempts to eclipse the present, he began to recall something of that lazy summer day and those that came after it. He *had* been alone with her only that previous afternoon, not in the car but sitting on one of the seats arranged at intervals around the sides of the lake, and in the other wood, the one on the hill overlooking the town, the dog running ahead of them as they talked while walking along. That had been real, hadn't it, even if these images of two people now belonged not so much to him but some other person, or persons, he was watching from afar. She also had those Mediterranean blue eyes like the girl he had picked up in the car the night before, and who, for some reason he called or thought of as Stephanie, as had Kate, of course, eyes the colour in the French flag, mirroring the eternal sea and sky. He had felt it then, not in the same way he now did as a sickness, but altogether different, as a charm and attraction that steals over you as music does, or the sun on your face when it suddenly comes out on a cold winter's day, its warm glow taking you back to a time and place where there is no beginning or ending, only a remembered longing that briefly reappeared as the water of the lake began misting over before him.

CHAPTER 5

With the experience of a previous conviction hanging over him, and with the unrelenting realisation he was sure to be caught, by going to the police as he had, Ted brought about his arrest sooner than later. The fear rigidly frozen inside him was as much about being hunted and the headlines and public awareness it entailed, as it was of going to prison; that at least was an outcome, an ending or finality, and not the ongoing hell he was having to live with now. He was fully aware of what would inevitably take place once the police found out where he was, as he knew they would, just as they had some years before. It could happen at any time, perhaps when you were having lunch or tea, or out shopping, or most likely, as was their habit, in the early hours around dawn when you were in bed and at your most vulnerable; unless they picked you up at the entrance to the flat, after waiting in a car, silently watching, your description in front of them, as had happened before. In any case, it was only a matter of time before the doorbell rang and you opened it to find one or two plainclothes officers standing there, and to hear those words carrying such a fatal, paralysing ring to them, "Hallo Ted, long time no see!" After which, the questioning at the station or at home would begin as they let themselves in to nose about in that way they had while undermining what false hopes you had left, exchanging intermittent looks or gestures like actors following the directions in a play. Strangers who knew all there was to know about you from enquiries and earlier records, they talked as if they had known you for years, as essentially they had, making the questions an explicitly personal matter, from which the rest of the world, and in some odd way, even yourself, was excluded, especially when your family, or in his case, his wife, knew nothing of, until society at large demanded to be told through the newspaper accounts of the subsequent trial. Crime, detection, punishment, were all part of a tacit, unwritten contract and agreement, in which everyone involved fed on each other in ever-decreasing circles, whirlpools, that became so small you always knew there to be no way out.

"This shouldn't take long sir, just routine enquiry," one of the two would say as they followed you through to the lounge, where they would glance about them in that curious, speculative way that somehow characterises their work.

"I hope so, I was just about to go out," you reply, crossing the room to the telly to switch it off. "What is all this about, anyway?"

"As I said, sir, just routine enquiry."

"Do you live here alone, sir?" the smaller of the two asks in a fairly amiable yet intrusive manner, wandering across to the window as he speaks.

"I'm married, if that's what you mean. My wife's at work."

"Are *you* in work, sir?" the first asks, seizing on this like a terrier as he glances down at the paperwork by the computer and turning over one or two pages with his hand.

"I'm self-employed," you say, somewhat defensively, having yet to make any money from it, from being at home in the middle of the afternoon watching television.

"So you have quite a lot of time to yourself, do you, sir?" the constant use of the word sir being their defence against any accusation that they have been heavy-handed.

"Yes, I suppose so," you reply, giving this some brief thought. "A certain amount when I'm not working."

"What kind of work do you do, sir, if you don't mind my asking?"

"I'm a freelance journalist and writer, if you must know," you say, pausing again. "I write articles, stories, that kind of thing," you add, wondering if one of them is about to ask you what these are and have they been published. But instead the smaller one undoes the assumption by hitting you where it really hurts as you then realise this had been but a softening up procedure.

"Do you have a car, sir? I thought that might be yours outside."

"Yes, we do have a car. My wife uses it more than I do," you answer, hoping by this to cloud the issue a little more.

"Uses it every day, does she?"

"No, not every day, just when she feels like. Why, she hasn't had an accident, has she?" you venture, violently hoping this isn't so while knowing they are there for that other purpose lodged precariously inside yourself.

"No, nothing like that, sir," the taller one smiles as he carries on playing the game with only the one ending. "Not as far as we know."

"You had me worried for a moment. Look," you eventually manage to say in a forlorn attempt to take some kind of initiative, "what is all this about? Why are you asking me all these questions?"

"May I ask where you were last night, sir?" the smaller of the two with the more abrasive tone and manner, cuts in, undeterred, swatting away what you've said as if you were a fly.

"I was here. Well, after I came back from evening classes, that is."

"What time would that be, sir?"

"I'm not sure. Oh yes, around nine-thirty, I think."

"And you can verify that, can you? You wife, I mean?"

"Yes, of course," you answer, the very words having an optimistic ring to them that is itself a delusion. "Look, what is all this about!" you say for a second time, prompted by an instinct telling you that even if it isn't the best means of defence, attack is better than nothing at all. "You can at least tell me what's going on, can't you!"

"Yes, sir," replies the one now at the far end of the room, turning towards you as if from some strange planet only now coming into full view. "We're sorry to put you on the spot like this, however, the fact is we're making enquiries about a local girl. Her body was found in a wood not all that far from here."

Closer now, their eyes merge to focus directly on you.

"But why... I mean, I don't see how it's got anything to do with me!" you reply, as the hole in the ground beneath your feet opens a little wider.

"Probably nothing at all, sir," he goes on diplomatic to the end. "But, obviously we have to follow up all the available lines of enquiry. I'm sure *you* can understand that, sir," he concludes, a meaningful, slightly threatening note entering his voice, and one the other takes up, pausing before he speaks.

"The thing is, sir, we've been looking through our records," he starts to say, hesitating before going on as he allows this to sink in. "You know how it is, sir."

"I see what you mean," you somehow stammer, flummoxed, as their eyes go on sinking into you, although, having been aware that revelation has been on the cards all along, you know you shouldn't be surprised. "But surely you don't think – "

"We don't think anything, sir," the darker, taller one butts in. "We're merely making enquiries, as we said a moment or two ago."

"And you think it has something to do with me, obviously. But that's crazy. Besides, what happened, happened a long time ago," you lamely protest, the words hanging emptily in the air, as they still would be the following day or the one after as the alibi you have given begins to drop like a noose around your neck as the sound of a car coming to a stop below the window makes you glance nervously at your watch.

"Is that your wife, sir?" one of them asks, going to the window to look out.

"Yes," you say, recognising the sound made by the engine.

"But I don't want to bring her into this if that's possible."

"I think it may be too late for that, don't you, sir?"

CHAPTER 6

"This *is* an odd one," Detective Chief-Inspector Richards was continuing to think as they drove back from the scene of the murder, and while acknowledging that it had all the hallmarks of paedophilia still couldn't come to terms with the lack of sexual involvement that helped to understand such crimes, if anything could, unless it was seeing them for what they were, basic drives that gave love such a bad name when they got out of control, as they so often did and would go on doing so if his experience was anything to go by. As yet he hadn't had time to look at anything more than the preliminaries of the investigation, let alone analyse or become acquainted with what Ted had to say, as up to now he hadn't said much at all, except give his name, age and address, and show them where the murder had taken place. In other words, *why* had he done it? Forensics were still getting things together in the slow, thorough way they had, even though they were certain they had under arrest the person who they had barely begun looking for when he had popped up among them like a rabbit out of a hat. He'd always tried to separate the villains, or crooks as they were once so quaintly called, from the weirdos who defied general understanding in that they did things so bizarre they often were unable to explain why. At least that's how it had been not so long ago, while now the bizarre had become so normal nobody was surprised by anything anymore. Villains, or crooks, were a dying breed who spoke a language he understood, and by comparison came across as being 'honest', putting their hands up when caught and "going quietly" for the most part once the lawyers and other dodgy characters had failed to help them reap the benefits and rewards of a foiled security job or building society hold-up inspired by the idea of a pleasant lifestyle in Spain or some other sun-drenched idyll. He had never as yet met anyone, who on being arrested, said, "Bang to rights, guv'nor," or

"It's a fair cop," but when he joined the force in London all those years ago, had met coppers, as they were nicknamed then, who had. Then again, despite the crime, you either liked someone or you didn't; being a matter of personal chemistry, there were occasions when you couldn't help yourself, and instinct or a hunch often played such a large part in this you had to be careful to avoid confusing bias with evidence. There were times, when on instantly taking a dislike to someone, it was then found they had been innocent of the charges laid against them, only to find yourself still taking an intense opposition to everything about them. It wasn't only the less attractive or prepossessing who could do evil, he had found, there always being a strange tendency to see the beautiful or good-looking – especially where a woman was concerned – as somehow being a more likely repository for the virtue he still stubbornly believed to exist in most people, even those who cut corners and ended up in police hands. But where did Edward, or Ted, fit into all this and the gallery of rogues and misfits he carried around in his greying head? At first sight, when he had spoken to him for a short time at the station, it had been to ascertain if the person sitting in front of him was some kind of joker or indeed the more serious nutter or maniac who had been responsible for the death of the girl, which it now appeared he definitely was, having taken them to the scene, and which naturally made things a lot easier so far as police activities were concerned. In other words, his part in the investigation was literally over before it had begun, the girl's parents had been informed and had still to identify the body, of course, now it had been removed and taken to the mortuary; and whatever forensics came up with was mostly irrelevant now a confession had been made and guilt ascertained, though kept intact as a matter of procedure just in case someone or other in the legal profession tried to talk their way around it. All that remained before locking him up and throwing away the key, as was sure to happen, was the statement to be taken, but Williams and Mason could see to that. All the same, he went on being puzzled and intrigued by this particular murder as he would have been by most crimes seemingly without motive or gain. On the one hand it seemed such a pointless, gratuitous act, but fortunately lacking the violence usually associated with lust and sexual gratification, would perhaps bring some comfort, however small, to the parents, though, paradoxically, this palliative to their grief may not be as welcome as it should be when they were also informed they were at a loss and without any reason why their daughter had died so randomly. Cursing Ted, and those like him, with a metaphorically, mystified shake of the head, he nonetheless decided to scout around and see what more could be unearthed before Ted appeared before a magistrate and taken elsewhere while the date for the trial was set. But he knew that even then, when you had all the facts, figures and explanations to hand, there would still be the one great big *why* underlining this one unless he could get to the bottom of it. "Funny old business, human nature," he went on telling himself as the car turned into the station yard and he only then became aware that the person so much surmising and conjecturing was about, had, head on chest, fallen asleep beside him. It was, indeed, a funny old business and one whose intriguing conundrum deepened further when, on looking into the details of Ted's earlier conviction he found on his desk, he learnt that although this involved another under-age girl, it, too, was also distinguished from many others like it in there being also an absence of sexual assault, and it had been this, along with his age that had been taken into consideration when a lenient sentence had been passed.

It was very odd, indeed.

CHAPTER 7

"Sir!"

They had just come in from the yard, when hearing the voice calling him from just along the corridor, Detective Chief-Inspector Richards turned to see the same young constable, who had earlier told him that someone owning up to the murder was at the desk, bearing down on him.

"I thought I'd better tell *you*, sir," he said, glancing towards Ted and back again, his voice lowered. "It's Mrs Green, sir. We contacted her like you said. She's been here for some time, sir."

"Right. Thank you. I'll be along now," he replied, turning to speak to the others who stood waiting for him. "You go ahead, I'll be along in a bit."

As the others move on, he then speaks to the constable, joining him as they move down the corridor together.

"Where is she now?"

"In the front waiting room, sir. She's in a bit of a state."

"Yes, I'd be surprised if she wasn't. Poor cow," he added, in a sympathetic, if direct, tone.

"I've left one of the women PCs with her."

"Good. Well done," he said, a thoughtful look coming into his face.

* * *

His eyes opening and closing intermittently, a tired, rumpled Ted sits slumped backwards in a chair in the small, windowless interview room. Facing him in their chairs on the other side of the table, Mason and Williams are as intrigued and puzzled by the person in front of them, as their boss is. Though not out of their depth, they are content to tread warily, hoping Ted will take the initiative, and, as with so many others, do all the talking himself, which shouldn't be too difficult seeing as the hardest part is out of the way. The recording machine is on although as yet nothing has been said other than the date and time and the names of those present. On the table before them are the small number of statement forms and a pen that Mason now picks up to toy patiently with in his hand. Not so long before it would have been a cigarette adding its own aromatic drama to the atmosphere, only he had stopped smoking some time ago, besides which smoking was forbidden in all parts of the station, even the canteen. Thinking something should be said, if not only to keep Ted awake, he gives his colleague a sideways look and shrug before starting.

"In the car you said you loved her, and yet – I mean, you don't usually go around hurting people you love, do you?"

A rhetorical aside as well as a question, he gives the man facing him a quietly searching look before sitting back in his own chair and gazing up at the ceiling before making the same point in another way. "You just don't, do you," he says, pausing, trying to be relaxed before following it up with another that has been perplexing all of them on the way to the wood and back. "I mean, what did she do to you!"

This again, is not so much a question demanding an answer as an oblique sense of impatience and protest coming out into the open, but getting no response from the silently bowed head of the figure opposite, it leaves him wondering, as he gives Williams another quizzical glance, if the person sitting there is even hearing, let alone listening, to what is being said. So that when Ted's reply does come after a longish wait during which he continues lightly stabbing the table with the point of the pen, Williams looking absently into space, it's not only the muffled sound of his voice, which has been silent for almost all of the time

24

he has been in custody, but what he says that comes as more of a surprise to their waiting ears.

"She hurt me, I suppose."

As he says this, there is a simple note of resigned protest in his voice, while at the same time it is directed not only to the officers but also to his own questioning of himself to what has happened. And this chance remark causes them to again glance meaningfully at one another, with Williams giving a facial shrug as if to say, "Don't ask me what he means, I give up!" But smelling something in the wind now that answers seems more forthcoming, Mason seizes on this as he leans forward more intent in a bid for clarification.

"How?" he begins, in a manner and voice that isn't unkind or strictly accusative, and which by choice of words has a friendly touch to it. "How could she hurt you, Ted? I mean, she was only a girl, wasn't she? Not big enough to hurt anyone, really," this in turn being followed by another lengthy silence before Ted again speaks in a low, soft voice.

"I told you, I don't know," he says, hesitating before going on to drag the words up from the bottomless fissures of a confused and contorted void posing as his mind. "By being herself I suppose," he adds limply, seeming to sink further into himself before saying, "I don't expect you or anyone to understand," muttering this last sentence as if it were so deeply personal, nobody but himself could ever begin to see what he means, and it has both officers lapsing tiredly back into their chairs as his head again slumps forward onto his chest in a state of abject, detached fatigue.

This was not something Detective Chief-Inspector Richards liked doing; of all the onerous duties and thankless tasks he had been called upon to execute in his long service, this was among the worst, not that dealing with the dead was ever easy, only that they were just that, dead, and without any further say in the matter one could only guess at what it might be. With the living, however, the wives, parents, and husbands left to deal with the unspeakable, as he often called it, presented himself and other officers with something you were never really prepared for even if you had done it a hundred times before. You had a vague idea what you were going to say, that never changed too much; what you didn't know or could only guess at, was the reaction and what you would do or not do, then. He now wished he hadn't rushed so impulsively into taking charge of this particular case, but he had, and as Mason and Williams were otherwise occupied, it had been left to him to round off the corners now that most of the other matters had been seen to, though he had yet to see the parents of the dead girl – Charlotte was her name they had been told – to offer his condolences in the wake of another officer giving them the bad news earlier in the day. As the senior officer investigating the pointless murder of their daughter, they at least deserved that. He was only thankful it hadn't been him breaking the news to them, but if it wasn't one thing it had to be another, he was telling himself as he moved along the corridor towards the waiting room at the front of the building, and which was exactly that, being like so many others of their kind in police stations, or dentists and doctors up and down the country. For no matter how busy they might be, you were always alone in one, weren't you, alone and waiting for good or bad news, although the very nature and atmosphere of such places inevitably made you fear the worst. And this medium-sized room he was about to enter was exactly what it was meant to be, a waiting room with a few chairs against the walls and a small table with a scattering of magazines standing in the middle of the uncarpeted floor, with only the lights of passing traffic glancing off the panes of frosted glass to tell you it was facing the road.

Sitting inside the door is a woman police constable, flicking through a magazine on her knee; sitting opposite her on the other side of the room is a tired-looking woman showing all the signs of edginess whom she knows as Mrs Green. As Detective Chief-Inspector Richards comes into the room, the woman police constable immediately puts down her magazine and jumps to her feet.

"Good evening, sir," she says, straightening her uniform and picking up her hat that had fallen to the floor.

"Evening," he replies in a pleasant, if brief, tone.

"This is Mrs Green, sir," she says, turning to him, her voice lowered. "I was sitting with her until you arrived."

His eyes take in the figure as she speaks, Anna, in turn, having glanced towards him on entering the room, now looks away again, lost in thought.

"How long has she been here?" he asks, emulating the quieter tone of the woman police constable.

"I'm not quite sure, sir. I've been with her for about an hour, though. She wanted to know why she was here, but I didn't tell her anything apart from saying it was routine."

"Has she had a cup of our famous tea?" he asks, and although there could be a trace of humour in this, it is said without any attempt at one.

"No, sir. I asked her if she wanted one but she said no." She paused after speaking, glancing across to the woman before turning back to him. "Do you want me to stay, sir?"

"No, I don't think so," he replies, giving her a smile. "Thank you."

"Thank you, sir," she says, pulling on her hat as she goes out, leaving him to move across the floor towards Anna, who starts to get to her feet, her mouth and lips already poised to say something.

"No, don't get up, Mrs Green," he says with what he hopes is an encouraging smile, leaning forward to pull a chair closer to where she is sitting. "It's been a long day and I'd welcome any opportunity to give these legs of mine a rest."

* * *

Anna, or Mrs Green, as Detective Chief-Inspector Richards came to know her, knew about scares. Even though it had turned out to be benign, on being diagnosed with cancer some years before meeting Ted, the unbelievable shock of this had prepared her for the worst. But there were no cures or remission for the dread that now engulfed her as she sat trying to take in the enormity of what the man who introduced himself as DCI Richards was telling her.

"Are you sure?" was all she could find to say at finding herself the last person left alone in the world to face the monsters now confronting her, and using those very same words when, after the results of her tests had come through after an agony of waiting, another man with a similar air of authority had told her there was no cancer and she had nothing to worry about. From that moment of suppressed relief to what she was hearing now, seemed only a step away as she tried to grasp the extent of what he was trying to tell her.

"Yes, we're sure," he was saying. "Ted has confessed to it and apart from that we have every reason to believe what he says. I'm sorry, I know this has come as a terrible shock to you," she heard, felt the words themselves piercing her as the man's mouth went on opening and closing as she began falling beneath a weight in which there was no room to move or breathe. How could it be Ted, said a voice that went on so repeatedly it was only this that told her it was her own, he was quiet and so inoffensive, he wouldn't hurt a fly, let alone do what this man was telling her he had. Maybe they'd got him mixed up with another person, someone with the same name, that happened, didn't it, they'd even sent people to prison who were then proved to be innocent. Tiny inklings of doubt without any real substance to cling onto, entered the swirling clouds of her confusion, and as rapidly left again. Her own personal hell, it had no doors from which to exit once those through which you had been pushed were closed for good. When she got the phone call asking her to get in touch with them, she had imagined it was perhaps concerning some kind of traffic offence Ted had incurred, and hadn't liked to tell her; better still, and more likely, maybe he had been a witness to an accident and they wanted him to give more details. Whatever it was that passed hurriedly among her scattered thoughts, after getting the call and then driving to the station, she had never, for one single second, envisaged it was anything like this. Why on earth should she, when Ted, for all his funny moods and erratic punctuality, had never given her the slightest suspicion he would have been capable of doing such a thing. It just didn't make sense.

In the interview room, head buried in arms on the table, a distraught Ted sobs with the regret and frantic despair of a child whose favourite toy had been lost or thrown away, went some way towards the two officers establishing a little more of his emotional vulnerability. Feeling they are at last getting somewhere, without quite knowing what, their attitude and expressions are showing a somewhat incredulous interpretation of what has been going on as they wait patiently for him to enlarge on the muffled words, punctuated by sobs, they have so far heard.

"I didn't mean to hurt her. I loved her," he says, not for the first time, the quiet conviction underlying the claim subsiding into another burst of remorseful sobbing joining one that hadn't

29

really gone away, other than being interrupted by these few, broken sentences.

"It's a bit late for that, old son, isn't it," Williams finally says, as the effect of the words faded away, his own expression one of a tired, and tiring, frustration. Nearing the end of his shift, he already had one foot in the more enjoyable hours ahead.

"I don't expect *you* to understand! I don't expect anyone to, do I?"

Said in the same resentful and aggrieved tone as his previous utterance, the inflection unconsciously expressed in these last two words hint at a secretive nature hidden so deep inside himself its fuller comprehension will only become clearer when he is far away from here.

*　*　*

"I didn't know, I had no idea..."

Her voice broken by an outburst of tears, a sadly bewildered Anna struggles for words while wiping her eyes. "I mean... he's always been... you know... well, normal in that way. There have been times when Ted's been moody and distant... but then, we're all capable of that, aren't we..." She pauses, dabbing at her swollen eyes with a handkerchief. "But I never would have imagined he would have done anything like this, though," she says, her voice fading away to break up into another eruption of tearfulness as she buries her face into her handkerchief.

"Yes, I know," Detective Chief-Inspector Richards is prompted to say, holding back and making allowances for her distress before speaking. "I think this is why such things always do come as something of a shock... it's always so well-hidden."

"I didn't even know about that other time you say he was in trouble," she replies in a hoarsely fatigued tone. "As you say, it isn't something you talk about, is it?"

She cries softly, gently, as he looks helplessly on, against his wishes or better judgement thinking this is perhaps as bad as it can get, and pleading with the invisible powers that be that it doesn't have to happen again, as the only words he can think of come into his head.

"I am very sorry... believe me..."

Awkwardly sympathetic, he looks away and then back again, wanting to help but unable to offer anything of real use other than the platitudes that crowded in on him when his wife had died, and which he now shuts his own mouth on as he knows they invariably fall on deafless ears.

"I wish I knew what to do," he hears her say, in a voice that is more of a sigh. "What do you do?" she asks, although he recognises this to be a cry or plea for help, rather than a question.

"Yes, I know," he says, the softer assurance he senses is needed at this point. "I know exactly what you mean, Mrs Green but if you want my honest opinion, in circumstances such as this there is really only one thing you can do, and that is to try and make a new life for yourself." He pauses, a certain commiseration again coming into his face and words as, not for the first time, he tries putting himself into her position. "Over many years in this job, I've come across this situation more times than I care to remember, and I've yet to come up with an alternative solution or answer."

As he speaks, his eyes leave her and then return from some other place in the room he doesn't recall seeing, in himself, while she, too, is staring vacantly down towards the floor, again lost in that other, brutally dislocating world that won't leave her alone.

"What will happen to Ted now?" she suddenly asks, her voice distant and remote, looking up as she speaks, the handkerchief clutched in her hand.

"I can't really answer that just now," he replies, allowing for a short silence before going on, as he carefully chooses his words. "That's for others to decide, I'm afraid," he adds, feeling uncomfortable as he says this, without quite knowing why.

"Will he be able to get some help?" she asks in the same distant, faraway tone.

"Possibly," he answers, his face taking on a small shrug. "It will depend on where they send him, of course," another interval of silence coming between them as she continues to wipe reddened, tired eyes.

"Where is he now?"

"We're just taking a statement from him."

"Is it possible for me to see him?"

"Yes, I don't see why not," comes the reply, along with a brief understanding smile, as he went on being grateful for finally arriving at this moment.

* * *

Although things in the interview room had failed to produce all the answers, they had at last got Ted's statement confessing to the murder when Detective Chief-Inspector Richards came into the room, a rather tentative, apprehensive Anna trailing behind him in the corridor.

"How are we going? Everything okay?"

"Yes, sir," both officers muttered, almost simultaneously as they got to their feet on seeing him, his own eyes switching from one to the other and taking in the crumpled figure of Ted in the same cursory sweep of the room.

"We're about finished," Mason said, taking the initiative. "We thought we'd wait for you, sir," Williams moving to switch off the recording machine after giving details about the time, and of Detective Chief-Inspector Richards entering the room, and then, picking up the statement from the table, following Mason to the door, where hovering in the corridor, they see Anna for the first time.

"This is Mrs Green," he says, standing by the partly-opened door. "I said she could have a few words with her husband. Wait for me outside, I won't be a minute."

As the two officers go out, giving her a customary look of appraisal, he ushers her forward, taking her arm and saying, "I'm afraid I can only let you have ten minutes or so."

"Thank you."

"You can have that cup of tea now, if you like?"

"Not for me, thanks," she answers, with an attempt at a grateful smile.

"How about you, Ted?" he says, looking across at the huddled figure giving a small, miserable shake of the head as he goes on shrinking into himself.

"If you ask for me, I'll have a car take you back if you like," he then says, addressing Anna.

"That's okay, thanks. I came in my own."

"Right," he says, in answer to this, turning to go. "If you want anything more, there'll be someone outside."

"Thank you."

As the door closes behind him, she then begins to cry as she moves towards the man sitting slumped in the chair, towards someone she loved and thought she knew so well.

"Oh, Ted, what's happened to you, darling!... Why? Why didn't you tell me..." she begins to say, the words spilling out in an anguished rush.

CHAPTER 8

Whatever else had been in his mind, Ted Green was never under any illusion or self-deception about the outcome of his trial and the length of time he would have to serve. Even with remission and any other advantages, at the earliest moment of release he would be in his mid-forties. It was a terrifying thought he had somehow managed to distance himself from during the various moves he was to make in the system, from police station, on remand, then wherever he was to be held while the trial took place. After that, once the sentence had been passed and there were no longer even the flimsiest of barriers standing between him and the isolating confines of the existence to come, it all came to a violent, self-defeating crunch the night he "lost it" as the jargon goes, and no longer able to stop the walls and ceiling of the cell crashing in on him, prayed for help from the blessed, if unholy, trinity of sheets, bed (to lurch from), and window bars, in an attempt to save himself from a fate far worse than any death: life.

Having then, as he was later told, been found by a vigilant member of staff and rushed to the prison hospital amid ringing alarm bells and the frantic hurrying of feet, a flickering, intermittent consciousness fused with a vague recollection of those last minutes in the cell, had left him wondering if this was a dream and he'd succeeded in what he'd set out to do. That is, until a vast groan of unbearable despondency at the misery welling up inside him instantly removed all vestiges of this when through opening and closing eyes, images, both near and faraway, of the bars at the window opposite, brought him back to the hell he'd thought he left behind. Suddenly, in and around his head, like a swarm of angry wasps, his own clamouring, dismaying voice was crying out, "So you're still here, are you, you fucking idiot!" as he went on cursing himself for ever having been stupid enough to think the ordeal was over when in a place like this everything possible was done to make sure nobody got away with it if it could be avoided. It was as though he *had* died, at least to himself, and then been brought back to life by some incorrigible god or other to live out a nightmare as bad, if not worse, then the one he had tried to leave behind.

Days later, drugged to the eyeballs as a precaution, he remained incapable of doing anything but staying in bed or sitting in a chair staring fixedly ahead or around him in surroundings that never failed to keep on reminding you of a situation that was impossibly hopeless, despite everything being done to "get you back on your feet" as Gordon, one of the nurses on the wing put it, as you were helped to put distance between yourself and the breakdown commonly known among prisoners as "stir fry" or "Chinese takeaway", phrases revealing a certain grim humour with regard to inmates who injured or tried to kill themselves. He wouldn't be the last and he certainly wasn't the first.

CHAPTER 9

Following the immediate shock and upheaval, it was only after the trial that Anna's gradual and fuller understanding of her husband's behaviour became clearer. It was then, in the aftermath, as the facts began to surface, both in her own mind and those forthcoming as the trial itself got underway, that she began to realise how little she knew about Ted, and that what she did know was not only far from being the truth but also at variance with the person himself, the disclosures as they filtered out becoming improbable and very sad. In this way, after her initial resistance to the idea, she had finally taken Detective Chief-Inspector Richard's advice about moving, her depression having played its own part in holding her back, while the very idea of selling the flat and going to live in another part of the country seemed too much of an ordeal. She had liked not only the flat but the town and area itself, but as the weeks and months leading up to the trial had gone by, this had slowly changed, and instead of hoping the shadows would lift and everything return to something like normality, it soon became more apparent that her emotional loyalty about staying where she had been happy was a mistaken one and that leaving was the only sure way of putting this nightmare behind her and in the past where it belonged. Even if she had decided to stay it would have become increasingly difficult as the publicity about the trial meant she herself had become the focus of unwarranted attention and speculation leading people to gossip and suggest that as Ted's wife she must have known about his behaviour all along. She had seen people in the street stopping and pointing out where the cause of so much upset had lived, and having had notes shoved through the letter box saying as much, she had thought of taking them to the police before thinking better of it. Anonymous as they were, what could they do except make things worse, and now she was moving it didn't seem to matter, anyway. On top of this, other residents in the apartment block where she lived, most of whom she barely knew except to say hallo to, had begun to avoid her, drawing back inside their doors when they had seen her coming, and so leaving her to assume they thought of her as someone who had shared his bizarre proclivities and interest in young girls, as the media had reported them. And, of course, although she had never for a second condoned what he had done, she had loved him and been happy living there, and which, in so many ways, she still thought of as her home and found little incentive or pleasure at the thought of starting again, not only in another flat or house, but also in a town or city where she would not only be alone, which she had never liked, but also a stranger.

The pivotal moment that helped make the final decision for her, came when, sorting through Ted's belongings as there were things to be sent to the prison, she came across the photographs in an old suitcase of his that had been on top of the wardrobe in what they used to call the cubby hole or boxroom. Along with them, and neatly folded in a plastic bag, was a school blazer that she thought must be quite old as it was faded and creased in places. Thinking this must have been kept out of sentimentality, she put it aside before, shaking the photographs from the large envelope they had been kept in and starting to sift through them, almost immediately the words, "Oh Ted, poor you!" came into her head on seeing the faces of teenage girls, dressed and undressed, staring out at her; some, which had obviously been cut out of foreign magazines, she put into the bin liner for the dustman, while keeping back other personal-looking ones which she thought could have been family photographs he would have wanted to keep. To help determine if they were, she checked the reverse of these for any writing that would help identify who they might be, noting that most of them were of a young girl called Susie at various ages in her life: her name, dates, and that of various seaside resorts on their backs, those of her smiling up at the camera from beside a sandcastle on the beach, or paddling in the sea, trousers rolled up, indicating they were taken on holiday or some similar occasion. Other photographs of teenage girls seemed to have been taken more recently, some in the local park as she recognised the lake and other features in the background, many of these were of a pretty blonde girl with a dog and the names Julie and Romeo written on the back. There was also a camera she didn't know he had, containing an undeveloped roll of film, these discoveries joining others in a list whose secrecy only added to her sadness and sense of loss. Coming across them was not only a complete surprise but further confirmation, if any were needed, not only of his deviousness, but also the way it dredged up memories of his behaviour and attitude towards her at various times, and leading her to question many things starting to come into her mind as it went back not only to the fateful day he had been arrested, but so many others before it. It had been like some human jigsaw in which bit by bit the parts were now coming together and which allowed her to recall how, when there had been a report of some sex crime or other on the television, or was part of a film being shown, he would get up and make some excuse for leaving the room. Or when they made love, which on reflection hadn't been all that often, he would insist on having the light off, saying it made things more exciting, and which she now saw fitted in with the girls he so blatantly preferred, if the fresh, nubile faces and bodies of the girls in the photographs were anything to go by, and which in turn made her think how old and less attractive he must have found her. Altogether, what she found in that old suitcase severed any remaining conjectures and ambiguities she may have had about Ted's activities, putting beyond all doubt that his obsessions and problems had been there all along without her realising it. There had been other occasions when, on looking back, she now knew had some meaning or other that wasn't quite right, and not as she had done, passed them off as moods or fancies without some more abnormal or unusual significance. She couldn't quite remember the day or week, but recalled how, when coming in from work, she had found Ted lying face down on the bed, convulsed with sobbing, his shoulders going up and down under the hand she put out to console him. He wouldn't tell her why this was and she didn't press him for an answer, thinking it had something to do with the frustrations he sometimes mentioned when he wasn't able to write the things he wanted to, seeing himself as a failure. What she wasn't to know was how grief-stricken he had been when Julie, the girl in the photos with the dog, had told him she and her parents were going away, just as she was to never know the extent of his friendship with her or any of the others smiling and gazing pensively out from the photographs she was putting aside, the last of these being those of another young girl sitting on the step of a caravan and waving happily towards the camera, the name Kate written on their backs.

Along with the photographs, there had been so many other things she couldn't put her finger on but which, in coming and going as they did, went on reminding her how in so many aspects of their relationship she had been rather like an over-tolerant mother hen having to keep a wary eye on an offspring venturing too near the road or the cat next door, reflections at which she now tried to smile, seeing it as the price to be paid when an older, mature woman lets herself become involved with a younger man. At the same time, she had felt herself so lucky to have formed this attachment rather late in her life than to have gone on feeling sorry for herself as she had been since the earlier divorce. But, having been shaken by the spate of such revelations, starting with her visit to the police station, and having now taken the decision to break with the past by moving on, she had dared herself to take a deep breath in thinking there could be little more by way of a surprise, when, paying her an impromptu visit not long after the trial was over, Detective Chief-Inspector Richards pulled one or two other rabbits out of a seemingly bottomless hat to mystify her even further.

CHAPTER 10

"How are we today, then? Slept well, did we?" Fortyish, a bit overweight, Gordon, the nurse on duty and a figure whose pronounced feminine shuffle and effeminate voice would look equally at home in a gay club or bar, waltzes into the room with a tray containing food. Placing the tray on the bedside cabinet, he leans forward, hands on the bed, gazing down at the body under the blankets whose eyes then flicker briefly open before closing again in a gesture of resigned defeatism.

"How do you feel?"

"Weird, as usual," comes the faint reply.

"You will for a while. Be surprised if you didn't, the stuff we've given you. Gave us quite a fright, you did," he says, turning to the tray. "I've brought you something to eat. It's kitchen to bedside service here, you know, and you don't get that everywhere, I can tell you. Come on, let's get you propped up, in a day or two you'll be out of here and back to normal."

"I know, that's what's worrying me," Ted says in a far from jokey manner but which Gordon inimitably turns to his own use.

"Ooh, not only young and handsome but a sense of the droll, too. My luck must be in," he laughs, placing a hand beneath Ted's arm to help lever him up onto the pillow. "I'm Gordon, by the way, the last of the Gay Gordons some say, and ready for a highland fling at any old time, would you believe."

"I'm not really hungry."

"Not hungry! After all the trouble Delia Smith downstairs has gone to! Of course you are, dear. Everyone has to eat, don't they?"

41

"So they tell me," Ted replies as an aside, his voice faint, as Gordon wheels the tray holder that goes across the bed into place.

"Ooh, get you, with a nice line in optimism, too. It's becoming just like the West End here, whatever next!" he says, pausing patiently as he puts the tray down within easy reach. "Come on, Ted, don't go all daft on me, for Christ's sake. Who do you think you are, Bobby Sands!"

"No, but I wish I was."

"Oh dear, we have got our Y-fronts in a twist today, haven't we. Must be the time of the month I wouldn't wonder. Personally, I don't have anything against anyone topping themselves, it's a free country and they do it often enough, but when they start talking about doing it when I'm on duty and spoiling my no-claims bonus, that's when I start putting my foot down, lovey," then adding in a theatrically contrite manner, his tone changing as his voice softened. "Now look what you've gone and done, upsetting poor old Gordon like that. Gives me such a turn."

"Sorry Gordon," Ted manages to say while trying to smile, looking up at him through half-opened eyes and not really seeing much at all but the endless future staring back at him.

"Say no more, dear. That's how you feel, I'm sure. But things change, you'll see. At least, for what it's worth, you don't have to pay income tax in here, let alone put up with all those hours in traffic jams getting to and from work. I can always feel one of *my* migraines coming on just thinking about it. Now what about this food, it will be cold by now."

CHAPTER 11

"I'd like to be on first-name terms with people, so would you prefer to be called Edward, Eddy or Ted?" the psychiatrist was saying, with a friendly open laugh, that took Ted rather by surprise. "I'm not at all that sure there are other alternatives but I'm sure you'll put me right, won't you."

"Most people call me Ted."

A neat, tidy office, its walls a clinical white like most of the hospital wing, he was sitting facing the psychiatrist on the other side of a desk taking up the centre of a not very large room. To one side was a couch-bed with a folded blanket where the pillow would be, while in a corner near an empty glass medical cabinet stand a number of oxygen cylinders. Good-looking, slim, with a fading holiday tan, not much older than Ted, and informally dressed in a pale grey suit rather than the usual white coat, everything about him reflects the youthful new face of his profession.

"Ted, it is then," he says, with another bright smile as he leans back in his chair. "I see you've been in the hospital, Ted, or sick bay as some call it," making an allusion to the suicide bid as he leans slightly forward to give the papers on the desk in front of him a cursory glance to jog his memory. "Still there, I believe?" he adds, sitting back in the chair again.

"I think they're sending me back to the main building tomorrow," Ted replies, his manner subdued, his neck still painful if he moves it suddenly, as he goes on wondering if he's made the right choice in being there.

When, at first, he'd been told he could see the psychiatrist, whose monthly visit was coincidental to his period of recovery, he didn't care all that much if he saw him or not, thinking of it as having to listen to pointless, irrelevant questions about why he had "done it", let alone trying to make the effort of thinking up answers that would seem to have explained themselves. In any case, he didn't have to, he knew that. Why did people drink? To get drunk, but nobody questioned that, did they, just as in prison nobody questioned the suicide if he got away with it. He hadn't put in a request so nothing could be expected of him, and in all probability he wouldn't have gone along with it unless it had provided a good excuse for a change of scenery for an hour or so, besides which, once his name was on the register it would also mean getting away from the general routine of the main building when the psychiatrist came each month. In this way, prison was perhaps the only place where illness or incapacity was seen optimistically, as it was this that then conferred certain privileges on the patient who for a time ended up in the relative comfort of the hospital, such an oasis being a welcome relief from the unremitting drabness and bleak atmosphere immersing the rest of the place. Only in prison could even a visit to the dentist be eagerly looked forward to, better still, should an operation necessitate a stay in an outside hospital, this was seen as the most luxurious of all "breaks" available to anyone considered fortunate to find themselves in that situation. These breaks, such as the one Ted allowed himself, occupied but an hour or so, but nonetheless were grabbed at as an alternative to the usual regime, where apart from the recreational period, you could, and often did, find yourself locked in a cell for twenty-three hours a day. Doors were still locked, that went without saying, but it allowed you to see other parts of the prison where you wouldn't normally go, and talk to someone different for a change. Ted wasn't expecting more, for how could anyone or anything do that now, apart from the medication plugging the holes through which he felt himself to be draining away into the desert of a senseless, demoralising future that seemed without end and which he went on wishing was over.

"I see," the psychiatrist was saying in answer to hearing Ted was going back to the main building the next day. "How do you feel about that? Are you up to it?" he asked, aware how often his hand went up to his neck.

"I suppose so. Haven't got any real choice, have I."

"I suppose you've seen the doctor, have you?" to which Ted nodded, before he went on. "Not altogether all that pleasant, is it, especially for someone like yourself, a young, intelligent chap, if I can put it like that. But as a psychiatrist and someone who is here to help you, I feel for you, Ted, I really do, and I want you to know there are certain therapeutic procedures that will help you in this, other than the medication I believe you are presently receiving. This apart, one can only sympathise with the emotions and feelings you are experiencing just now, on top of the panic attack you've had. You feel alone... cut off from family and friends... your freedom has been taken away, and for some time now the world has been shaking its fist at you and saying how bad you are. That life is suddenly so very different to how it had been not so very long ago..." His voice tailed away as he gave the person sitting opposite him another encouraging smile. "Let me put it like this, Ted. The reason why I am talking to you in this way is not only to break the ice between us and to let you know I'm your friend – I'm not here to point the finger at you, as I said a moment ago – these things do happen in the best of families – but to try and help you see that what you *are* feeling now will in time go a long way towards that necessary acceptance we'll talk about some other time. But it is, in fact, the only way *to* deal with all this, otherwise bitterness and even remorse – whatever other virtues it may have – can eat you away, and the results of something like that happening can be very severe indeed." He lets out an agreeable laugh. "And we don't want that happening, do we, on top of everything else. This, I feel, is why you should continue with the tranquilisers at this stage – for a while, anyhow – and then see how things go on from there." He paused, scanning the other's face in order to try to ascertain how this was going, before continuing. "I mean," he paused again, "on the one hand I realise all this must seem pretty awful to you at this moment, and as I said earlier, this is to be expected, but what we have to ask ourselves – and try to prevent – is that you don't become any worse. I'm sure you wouldn't want that, would you," he said, giving Ted an expectant glance, and although not a question as such, waits for this to register.

"No," Ted, replies, giving a subdued shake of the head, his mind going back to that earlier kind of insanity he'd known even before he tried to end things.

"No, of course you wouldn't, who would. Which is why I feel the essential part of any help we *can* give you lies in your own efforts to understand not only those feelings and emotions upsetting you now, but also those underlying reasons for your being here. I realise this isn't easy for you, but if it's any help at all I really *do* think that being here – no matter how unsettling this must be – is immensely preferable to being outside and finding yourself in a position where you are again subject to those needs and desires that led to your conviction. Does this make sense?" he added, the tone of his voice and the brief pause that came before saying them, coinciding to emphasise the meaning placed on the words.

"Yes, sir," Ted answered, slowly nodding.

"Good man," said the psychiatrist, giving him another smile. "I'm sure there are certain areas we could possibly help you with, Ted, and I have to say I find your case, if I may put it like that, to be very interesting. But for now I think we should put much of this aside until you are in better shape, at which time we can go into this rather more thoroughly, as I'm sure there's already enough for you to have to deal with in one way and another." Stopping, he leaned forward to jot something down on a slip of paper. "You can see me at any time, of course, my visits permitting. On average, I come about once a month, so if you put in a request we can then have another chat. What do you think, will you do that, Ted?"

"Yes, I think so," he replied, as the words went on buzzing in and out of his head due to the effects of the tranquilisers.

"Good, I'll make a note of it," the psychiatrist said, again leaning forward to write on the same slip of paper. "I really do hope this little talk has been of some use to you," he said with a knowing laugh. "Gets you out of the sick bay or your cell for a while, doesn't it. Think about it, anyway. As I say, I think it certainly would be helpful to you if we do go a little more deeply into things. Perhaps on my next visit if you feel up to it. Meanwhile, I'm sure the staff here will continue to do their best for you."

As he is speaking, he gets to his feet, holding out his hand for Ted to shake. "It's been nice meeting you, Ted. I only wish the circumstances were different, that goes without saying, I hope. I know how difficult it must be to remain positive, if not exactly cheerful," he says, following Ted towards the door, "but do try to keep some kind of balance if you can, and then we can go on from there. It's really a matter, I suppose, of taking one step, one day, at a time, something that applies to all of us of course, in one way and another."

CHAPTER 12

"Gimme, gimme, gimme... a man after midnight..."

Giving one of Abba's songs his own particular emphasis, Gordon swans into the room carrying items of clothing over an arm. He pulls up short at Ted's bed, where the latter sits, legs dangling over the side a small suitcase opened on the bed beside him. It's the day after his meeting with the psychiatrist and although still on medication he is being moved back to the main building.

"Here are your other things, Ted. I dried your towel off."

"Thanks Gordon," he says, getting to his feet, unsure if it's the drugs or a deeper malaise putting him off-balance.

"So you had a good chat with him, did you?" Gordon asks as he begins folding the clothes to put them into the case. "Lucky old you, show me a couch and he can untie a few knots for me whenever he likes." He stops to look around him, taking in the bedside cabinet, radiator, and bed itself. "Have you got everything now?"

"I think so. Haven't got much *to* get, anyway, have I."

"Don't worry, you'll soon have the rest of your things sent on. And don't forget what I said, take it easy over there. Do as you're told, and whatever you do, don't let them see you looking resentful. In their eyes that's as bad as being too cheerful, and that would never do, would it," he says, locking the case. "Just go with it, okay? Trust Gordon, I've seen it all before, lovely."

CHAPTER 13

Having on a number of occasions seen the estate agent's sign outside the flats, it was only when the 'SOLD' notice appeared that Detective Chief-Inspector Richards overcame any hesitation he might have had on calling in on Anna. After all, he was part of the team instrumental in having her husband put away, and there were quite a few people who didn't take too kindly to that, or policemen generally. So thinking twice about parking his car in the spaces reserved for residents only, he left his further down the road before walking back to the block.

In the flat itself, things were in some disarray, with all the signs of someone packing up the contents prior to a move indicated by the tea chests and cardboard boxes, some full, some partly so, standing about the room. To an outsider this may have been seen as confusion, but to Anna's recent oscillating mental state it meant that things were looking brighter and more positive now that the main step, the selling of the flat, had been achieved.

Hearing the doorbell and having gone to answer it, she was taken aback, more than displeased, to see the man she had last seen at the police station on that dreadful night she was still unable to completely erase from her memory.

"I'm sorry to barge in on you like this," he said, following her along the corridor. "But I saw the sold notice outside and my curiosity got the better of me. I hope you don't mind."

"You'll have to excuse the chaos," she replied, going through to the lounge. "I'm in the middle of packing, as you can see." She gave a little laugh at the state of the room. "You don't know how much you have until you put it all together, do you."

"Go ahead, don't let me get in the way."

"There's no real hurry," she went on, removing various items from the chairs. "I'm not going until next week. Let me move these books so you can sit down."

"Thank you," he said, feeling a little better now that she had invited him in, when he could have received the kind of reception he'd at times faced in the past when doors had been slammed in his face. You just never knew in situations such as this.

"Can I get you anything to drink?" she asked, moving some clothing draped over the back of a chair.

"Not for me, thanks. Don't let it stop you, though."

"I've just had one, thanks," she answered, making room on the sofa for herself.

"So you are moving then. I saw the sign outside some time ago and assumed it must be you."

"Yes, finally. There seemed no point in staying once the trial was over. I think that's one of the things that helped me make my mind up. I'm going to live in Bristol, the firm I work for have an office there." She paused, her mind elsewhere. "They've been very good to me."

"Good, I'm very pleased for you," he said, hesitating before going on. "I notice you weren't in court, not that I was so surprised."

"Yes, I couldn't afford to take any more time off. Not that I would have enjoyed the proceedings, I'm sure."

"That's understandable, I suppose."

"I went to see him at that remand centre, you know. I couldn't face that again. I know it must sound very selfish."

"No, not particularly. I've known many women who have felt the same, wives especially. It seems to be different with mothers, they usually stay in touch, it seems."

"It was after seeing Ted that the idea of moving came to me, although looking back it seems inevitable now. You were right, one has to try and make a new life for oneself, hard though it may seem."

"Yes, I'm afraid it is the only way, given the circumstances," he replied, before going on. "Did you follow it in the papers?"

"No," she said, shaking her head. "Not really, just some of it when it was on the television news. Obviously, Ted needs help, but I knew they'd make him out to be some kind of monster, I know what they're like." Unable to prevent a note of concern entering her voice, she paused before going on. "How is he? Have you seen him?"

"No," he said, shaking his head. "But in any case, I think he'd already made up his mind about the outcome of the trial so it was no real surprise, I'm sure. On the other hand, he'll be better off where he is, they have people who know about these things."

"I do hope you're right. He'd been knocked about when I saw him."

"It does happen, I'm afraid. That's why I say he'll be better off. It's not quite like prison, despite the locks and bars."

"Poor Ted," she said after a moment's reflection. "I still have difficulty coming to terms with all this, you know, and the way things can turn out. I suppose you never do stop asking yourself why or trying to figure out what went wrong, do you. There are still times when I can't help thinking I'm somehow to blame, and telling myself I should have known something was wrong," she said, her voice finally fading away into a temporary silence before then adding with a wry attempt at a grin. "So much for female intuition."

"I don't see how you can attach any blame to yourself. And if it's any help at all, I haven't yet met anyone in your position who hasn't felt the same."

"I even thought of contacting her parents to say how sorry I was."

"I shouldn't bother if I were you. They wouldn't thank you, not at this moment in time, anyhow."

"Such a waste of life," she said, pondering. "Both his and that poor girl's."

"I couldn't agree more. But this idea that you are somehow to blame for what happened, is one you should really try to put out of your mind. If the truth be known, Ted had a problem, or problems, long before he met you. That's shown by his earlier conviction, of course."

"Yes, I know you're right," she replied, with a thankful smile. "It's just that I think it's such a shame he wasn't able to get some help much earlier, then perhaps none of this would have happened." She gave herself another thoughtful smile before continuing. "He's always been insecure and rather moody, I knew that when I first met him. I think that's why he was attracted to me, an older woman. You know, he once told me that he didn't get on with younger women, those more his own age. He said they were confused and neurotic," she went on, another wry smile accompanying the words. "That's almost funny, isn't it?"

Seeing she was about to say more, he responded to this with a smile of his own, leaving her to go on.

"I suppose losing his parents when he was younger couldn't have helped, could it. Being an only child *and* an orphan too."

"Yes, there's a lot in what you say," he said, nodding in agreement. "However, as for being an orphan, that isn't strictly true," he added, giving her an enquiring look. "And from what we know, he wasn't an only child. Did you know he had a sister?"

"No," she answered, showing this. "You do surprise me. I always thought he was an only child. He never talked about having a sister."

"Oh yes, he had a sister, alright. Her name was Susie. I believe she died in a motoring accident when she was... thirteen, I think."

"Poor girl... how sad. But now that you mention it, Ted was always very vague about his background, quite secretive, in fact." Surprise in the form of a facial shrug, coincided with her words. "I never really asked him much about his past because I thought it upset him talking about his parents dying like they did when he was so young. But as for having a sister..."

Her voice trailed away in quiet disbelief.

"The mother died fairly young, and after a time they apparently went to live with a grandparent when the father couldn't cope. We know this as we managed to track down a neighbour of hers. She's dead now, the grandparent, I mean. I think his father may still be alive, but as he hasn't been in touch with us or Ted I can't be certain. Ted wouldn't say. Maybe he doesn't know. His father remarried, and after Ted was arrested on the abduction charge he and the new wife never had anything to do with him. I don't think she and Ted got on, anyway. It may well be that he resented her taking the place of his mother like that."

"So he wasn't an orphan?" she said, still surprised at the news.

"Well, being so young when his mother and sister died, then losing touch with his father, I think Ted saw himself like that, as being one, I mean. I'm sorry if this has upset you," he said, noticing her expression and how she had become quiet and not a little withdrawn. "But I thought you'd like to know."

"Thank you," she said, from somewhere inside herself, and giving him a brief, winsome smile, before saying, "You seem to know far more about him that I ever did."

"Well, it is part of our job to look into things, at the same time I have to admit that Ted's case did hold a special interest for me. Actually," he started to say, hesitating before going on, "much of this has only just come to light. I'm sorry if it's been something of a shock."

"Yes, it's certainly been that. I had no idea." She became quiet again, speaking as if to herself. "I wonder why he never spoke about her, his sister, that is."

"Maybe he found it too painful to talk about. One can only imagine what it meant to him at the time. By all accounts, they had been very close after their mother passed away."

"He must have been very lonely, mustn't he," she said, almost absently, trying to put herself into his shoes. "I think this is why it's been so hard for me to do what I'm doing, going away, I mean. After all, I am the only family he has from what you say."

"You can always write to him, you know," he replied, following a longish pause.

"Yes, I know. I had a letter from him just before the trial, but I haven't written back yet. There doesn't seem to be very much one can say."

Her voice drifts sadly away, leaving a silence that still manages to reverberate with all that's been said about someone whose image, though invisible, has somehow remained present in the room. Throughout the conversation, she'd tried to go on reminding herself of the terrible thing Ted had done, and yet, as it is with cigarette smoke that goes on persistently lingering after a party, she still couldn't entirely forget what had gone before, and all the nicer things about him.

"Good heavens, is that the time," he said, breaking the spell of her thoughts as he glances at his watch. "I must be off."

Getting to his feet, Anna does the same.

"I'm sorry to have kept you," she says. "But thank you for coming, it was very kind of you."

"That's okay, if anything it's me who should be apologising for keeping you from your packing. I was just passing when I saw the sign."

"I'll show you out."

"Oh yes, before I forget," he says, turning to her. "Do you happen to know anyone by the name of Julie or Juliette? A friend or relative, perhaps."

"Julie..." she replied, quizzing herself as she stopped by the door. "No, I don't think so. Why do you ask?"

"No special reason, it was just a name that came up somewhere along the line. She may not even exist, in all probability something of a fantasy Ted made up, who knows..."

It was only later, after he had gone, that she remembered the photographs she had found in the suitcase and the names Julie, the fair-haired girl with the dog, and Susie, who was obviously his sister, on the backs of them. Now she knew who she was, she wanted to look at them again, but as she'd already sent them on to the prison with Ted's other things, it was too late to do so.

CHAPTER 14

Ted didn't like Chapman, at the same time he didn't care all that much about any of the others even when there wasn't anything distinctly bad or obnoxious about them to dislike. Like himself, they were individuals who had done something for which they were being punished, and in prison it was only someone looking for trouble who made distinctions about who was good and who bad. But Chapman was someone he'd taken an immediate dislike to; no sooner had he left the hospital and been back in the building than he was upon him like a terrier with a rabbit, hanging about his cell at break or finding him at his elbow at mealtimes to ask about Charlotte and what she'd been like in that furtive way he found coarse and vulgar. With media coverage of their trials preceding them, most newcomers ran the same gauntlet to become the centre of attention, but only an occasional oddball like Chapman went endlessly on and on in wanting to know explicitly more about the details than had been reported. And Ted was no exception, particularly as he had caused so much trouble when being rushed to the hospital before reappearing so enigmatically among them a week or so later as someone who had cheated death. In achieving this, you attained a certain notoriety that took you beyond criticism or reproach for what you had tried to do, at the same time nobody praised him or said they were glad he had survived. Chapman being an exception, others picked up what they could more indirectly, in passing, as it were, hearing about things second-hand and through the grapevine of gossip. "Heard about the case, tough shit!" Or, "Hope they treated you okay, could do with a week or two over there, myself!"

In this way, at least with some, each newcomer was like a book to be briefly taken up, before being replaced on the shelf in favour of another arrival, and as on the outside, men attached and formed themselves into friendships and groups according to not only their personal chemistry but often more pertinently to those deeds and proclivities that had brought them there, and were mostly to be seen in twos or threes huddled together as an expression of some conspiratorial mutuality with only the occasional laugh to intrude upon the low undertones in which they conversed. Inevitably, there were, of course, those who sat alone for the most part, often with their heads in their hands as they suffered the torments and tribulations of hindsight and who rarely said anything unless they were first spoken to. Inward-looking, and, Anna apart, a loner with few close friends, in identifying with them Ted wasn't about to change the habit of a lifetime by including himself within any of the groups or alliances dotted about the recreation area when not in their cells.

Known colloquially as 'suicide watch' he was in one of the cells reserved for those considered to be a danger to themselves. The dreams and nightmares he'd known for much of his life continued, so that when he invariably awoke from a fitful sleep to find some disaster or other hanging over his bed, he was often too afraid to close his eyes and laid helplessly staring up at the ceiling as he tried to decide if where he was was real, or if it belonged to an unending horror story that in never going away would leave his mind constantly open to so many of those other apparitions queuing up to fill it.

The belongings Anna sent on had arrived when he was in the hospital, and after the material poverty he'd known since his arrest, having the clothes and books with him became another of those fragile lifelines that went some distance towards keeping bits of you afloat even when the rest was sinking. Ironically, among them were the notepads and a textbook he had used in his French evening class; then he was thing to conjugate verbs, now it was a conjugation of a far more serious nature he was trying to find a way around. He tried to laugh. Among the items, she'd enclosed a card saying she was sorry, and which made him cry as he read it and again later that night when he was in bed going over the recent past and what he had left behind.

It was as he was unpacking and sorting out the contents of his old suitcase and a box of books that one of the prison officers came to say the governor wanted to see him. "Must be your lucky day, Green," the man said, his sardonic, mocking tone being another of the many instances he and the others got a crude satisfaction from when putting in the verbal boot. On seeing his suitcase, hadn't one of them already remarked, "Bit soon for your holidays, isn't it?"

CHAPTER 15

"I hear things haven't been going too well, Green?"

"No, sir."

"What seems to be the trouble? Still depressed are we?"

"Yes, sir."

"Have you see the doctor, since your stay in the hospital, I mean?"

"No, sir. Only the psychiatrist when I was there."

"You found that helpful, did you?"

"Yes, sir."

"Good. I realise it can't be easy for you, but a problem shared is a problem halved, as I like to think."

"He said I would be able to see him on his next visit, if I wanted, sir."

"Yes, of course. I'll see that an appointment is made for you. Has your wife been in touch?"

"No, sir. I wasn't expecting her to."

"Yes, I remember you saying as much when I last saw you. That's a pity, however, my main reason for seeing you today has, I feel, quite a lot to do with your general behaviour and these setbacks you have been having. I am, of course, referring to the photographs found among your possessions when they arrived. Also the letters you have been writing to this girl, who, I assume, is the one you were very friendly with. I believe you were very fond of her dog?"

"Yes, sir."

"For obvious reasons, following a complaint from her family, we could not allow later ones to be subsequently delivered, even when the contents are as innocuous as yours appear to be. Is there anything you wish to say about this?"

"No, sir, not really."

"Although I think I can understand something of the need behind this, I feel the compulsion to contact her is far from being a healthy one, all things considered. One can see that you felt very deeply about her, while at the same time one must recognise that there is, as I'm sure you yourself will agree, no real point in pursuing this line of thought any further, is there. It cannot lead anywhere, can it, and naturally the one or two letters that did reach the girl she found to be quite disturbing, sad as this may seem to yourself. If you want my opinion, Green, such activities can only lead to a deeper sense of isolation and dejection, and so with this in mind I think it would be a good idea if you mention this to the psychiatrist when you next see him. Will you do that?"

"Yes, sir."

"How are you getting on with the other men? I hear you were quite friendly with Johnson?"

"Yes, sir. I didn't see much of him but we seem to have got on quite well."

"Yes, Johnson, as a good sort. What happened was a great pity. That must have been quite upsetting for you?"

"Yes, sir. It was when I heard about it."

"Well, try to put that behind you as best you can. These things happen, but I'm sure you will get to know others with similar interests to your own as time goes by."

"Yes, sir."

"Well done. Yes, I think that's all for now, Green. Oh yes, before I forget," he said, pausing to take from a drawer in his desk a large envelope and pushing this towards him. "I think these are yours. I have no objection to what you choose to write as long as you do not send it outside. Nonetheless, although I cannot allow you to keep the photographs of this girl called Kate, I see no real harm in your keeping those of your sister and other members of your family, provided you take good care of them. They may so easily fall into the wrong hands and I'm sure you wouldn't want that. I'm sorry these were taken from you when your belongings arrived, the officers were only doing their duty, as I'm sure you'll understand."

"Yes, sir, thank you."

"By the way, I was surprised and rather sad to read in your report that you lost your sister when you were a boy?"

"Yes, sir."

"Yes, I was very sorry to hear that she died as she did, very sorry indeed. How old was she?"

"Thirteen, sir, three years older than myself."

"Such a pity. It must have been very hard for the family and yourself."

"Yes, sir, it was. We were very close, she used to be very protective towards me."

CHAPTER 16

Having his own things around him, gave Ted not only a feeling of comfort in a cell where this was the last of all considerations, but which also opened a small window to let in some light and colour from the outside world. Sorting through his belongings, he couldn't help but hold some of them up to his face and so savour a little of that past trembling in his eyes and hands, however quickly this passed once the clothes were put away and the books neatly arranged against the wall on the table. It was but another of those small breaks or stratagems to be thankfully grasped, like being taken to the governor's office through a meandering river of corridors, or seeing the psychiatrist, as he was down to do in a few days. One lived for such opportunities in getting away from the confines of the cell, and died when they weren't there. Whereas he had initially found the night light above the door as irritating as the knowledge his 'wellbeing' was checked at intervals by someone surveying him through the spyhole in the door, he was now grateful to the former in making it possible to see so that he could write in his notepad when he could no longer get to sleep. This had meant sleeping in another position with his head towards the door, for which he had to obtain permission. They came down on you like a ton of bricks if you stepped out of line over the slightest thing, but if you asked nicely a change such as this was usually granted. In truth, this is what being in prison really meant, not only the loss of your freedom but also the natural inclination to think and act for yourself unless permission was first sought. But on suicide watch the main 'perk' lay in having a cell to yourself and not having to share one with someone like Chapman, the very notion that he had somehow managed to avoid this and have his own small space, resulting in a self-congratulatory pat on the back as a reward for the bruising to his neck and what had gone before.

Waking in the night, or in the early hours as he had a habit of doing, he would automatically reach out for the notepad and pen he kept by the bed, and by the glow above the door, start jotting down the thoughts and feelings that came to him. It was not only an alternative to just lying there and letting the demons riot in your brain, but the only option left trying to comprehend how he'd got into this mess by pulling together the strands of what he'd so thoughtlessly done without regard to its consequences. He *had* killed someone, he *was* in prison, he *had* tried to kill himself, and from that terrifying instant when she had stopped breathing, contrition and remorse had underlined his waking consciousness. Fearful that the insanity possessing him might then cause him to do something like it again, he'd been driven to go to the police. He'd never hurt anyone before, let alone become violent; bullied at school, he hadn't even retaliated and used to run away with shouts of coward pummelling his ears. If being in prison was an altogether worse mess than the one before, on looking back at it he couldn't help but breathe a sigh of some relief at being in prison and further away from the madness that had filled him then. If anything, he'd loved Charlotte, she had been so beautiful, she still was beautiful in the small picture frame of her he carried in his head: *too* beautiful, really. Sometimes she appeared at the very end of an inexhaustible list of experiences and images that came and went in his mind as he wrote them down, while at other times she was at or near the beginning of these regurgitated memories dredged up from their inexplicable, unaccountable past. At first there had been some vague notion of driving her around all night, or of taking her to some place where they could have talked and been alone. At the trial he'd mentioned this, or tried to, but the moment he found himself with her the idea vanished, giving way to feelings of a different nature. He wasn't so alone then. But although he hadn't set out to harm her, nobody believed it at the time anymore than they did now, and this in itself, this misunderstanding, made everything that much harder to explain. It hadn't been planned or premeditated, as they tried to say, giving a cold, detached logic to their account in contradiction to his own. It *had* just happened, as things do, and nothing *could* change or alter that.

Scribbling away in the notepad at all hours, day and night, the pen was a needle injecting regular antidotes for the relief and abatement of a despair brought on by the incessant beating of one's head against a hopelessness as dense as the walls themselves. Telling himself he'd never get used to it, to being there, he came to an irrational conclusion in thinking of the cell not as an opponent or enemy to be fought and escaped from but as an entity he should familiarise himself with more intimately by running his fingers over its shiny, painted brickwork, and in so doing, in forming a deeper acquaintance and understanding with this impregnable surface, minimise the threat it held by reducing each of the bricks into numbers and single units as opposed to the one solid, unyielding mass. This was how, rather than go on restlessly twisting and turning in a broken sleep, he found himself at one point standing on the bed and stretching upwards in the half-light in an impossible attempt to count the bricks in the highest sections, in this way giving another slant or meaning to a much-used prison expression, "It had me climbing up the wall, man!" it not taking too long in coming to realise how such exercises in inane folly only exacerbated the misery to be breathed in when the cell door next slammed shut and you were once again face to face with that most persistently ravenous of all predatory wolves, isolation, its mouth opened as it lay in wait ready to consume you. There were many illusions to be juggled and then thrown aside when 'stir fry' took hold of you, but only the one truth, the only honest answer to the perennial question, "How do *you* do it, man, how *do* you pass the time?" being, "By going quietly mad, what else!" And although he thought he understood why Anna had included a calendar that came in the box of books, just seeing the mountain of dates barring the way to freedom proved so discouraging that after keeping it for a day or two he then threw it away.

Some men had calendars in their cells in which they solemnly ticked off the passing days and weeks, often running ahead of themselves when it was applicable by placing a circle around the day of release or possible parole. For others, no calendar or sense of time could encompass an eternity that when it did finally come to pass some twenty, thirty, or forty years later, meant also a collision with two other planets beckoning from afar, old age and death. For them, and for Ted to a lesser, if still onerous degree, the only way forward if one were to survive and retain a semblance of sanity, resided in anaesthetising themselves to a reality so far into the future all they could reasonably look forward to or be content with were the benefits immediately within reach: a fag, visit, game of table tennis or snooker, a newspaper if you could get to one before it vanished or became irretrievably ripped apart. An ineradicable part of a sentence, and one best summed up both glibly and fundamentally in the phrase, "If you can't do the time, don't do the crime," came from the heart-stopping moment of stepping from the van into the heavy, unrelenting atmosphere of the prison building, time as such comes to a savage standstill, as you go on asking yourself can you have only been there a day when it seems like a month.

Around this time, on one of the many nights when only erratic, short-lived spells of sleep were possible and he was awake listening to the intermittent breaks in the mostly impenetrable silence of the building, he wrote: Four o'clock. Huddled over these pages, I write: *obsession*, a prison cell waiting to close its doors on you, a notion that with a kind of posthumous clarity has occurred to me a few times since I've been here but only now becomes solidified into all-knowing words, along with these

65

others gleaned from a reference book borrowed from the library. *To haunt, beset, trouble, preoccupy the mind*, to which, in the irrevocable hell of hindsight and impossible to overlook, are added, *separation, remembrance*, ruefully joining hands on a list which in any case soon loses any hope it had of being anything more. Dictionaries and their like, giving nothing more than a blandness to any meaning or definition of what I want to say, all fall short of that compulsion urging you to follow, however blindly, a love that has lost its way, or got out of hand as someone or other described it at the trial. Infiltrating each breath and pore, and from which there is no chance of recovery or reliable cure, those puzzled, bewildering longings that led here are also integral to a yearning forgetfulness hanging above one's head like a noose that takes the breath away. While, of course, there is more than one kind of death or dying, as many of us who find their way here soon come to realise. Behind bars, the idea of longevity quickly loses any affinity to that virtue accorded it in that other reality known as the outside world. Here pursued and harried by the errors of a previous existence, and by the dreams of an irreconcilable terror lying in wait for them – another reason why sleep is so hard to come by – the nights are invariably punctuated by the cries and stifled screams echoing from the monstrous, unearthly depths of a landscape that even in daylight lets loose horrors that have escaped the dark so as to go on alarming in other inescapable, frightful ways. On the march, the cries of the dead would not be out of place, for they, too, would go unheeded among spectral visions of lost freedoms that rise up and vanish with numbing predictability as they spell out minute by frenetic minute the days, weeks, months and years to be suffered with the face pressed hard against tears growing cold on pillows that have no comfort or solace to offer.

CHAPTER 17

"Get yourself ready, Green. Your turn for the shrink. It's all fun and games for some, I dunno how you do it."

He'd been trying to catch up on sleep from the night before, when the key turned in the lock and the voice following it got him to his feet and reaching for the shoes by the bed as the door swung open. Then, falling into step alongside the officer, they were back in that same luminous river of polished corridors, the overhead lighting streaming off the walls and floors someone had been mopping down earlier that morning.

One, two three, four... he was counting the steps, the length of time it would take to reach the hospital wing, his own not as long or quick as the officer's, so he was a stride or two behind him, conscious of the man's black shoes with their thick rubberised soles that made little noise, the silver glint of the bunch of keys welded to his belt giving out a metallic ring as they came to the first of the locked doors waiting to meet them. He went through first as was always the way, the officer stepping aside after opening it, to wait for him on the other side, as it was then locked in a routine or procedure established as soon as you got in the place. It wasn't unlike the army in that you followed by example. As they moved on he felt like saying something as a reply to the barrier between them, but then thought better of it, his tongue stilled in his slightly open mouth, the inclination frozen almost as soon as it came to him. Best to wait until he was spoken to, and in any case this one had already shown his antipathy towards him, towards the nature of his conviction, without even saying a word, you knew that from day one. Then again, what would he have said, something totally stupid and banal, no doubt, the idea mostly arising because he hadn't spoken to anyone but one or two of the other inmates since the day before, preferring to keep his silence at what was called breakfast earlier in the day.

One, two three... having lost count he started again, the proximity of the officer prompting things to come into his head as he went on being not a little jealous and envious of the man's ability to finish work for the day and then go home in his car or by bus to his house and garden, wife and children, cat or dog, to be able to leave the rigidity of the place behind as he entered that other magically pulsating universe outside the walls and perimeter fencing. Along with other officers, he was from another galaxy and a race apart, for not only had he been given the means to dictate the lives of lesser mortals such as himself, but had been granted the power to walk through doors and walls whenever he wished and to wander the earth at will.

Coming to another door, the large, smoothly burnished key, in again becoming the sorcerer's wand, instantly transmuted the edifice into another yawning corridor, the gleam of light playing on the spectacles of an approaching officer momentarily turning them into a twinkling star as he stepped aside to let them pass, giving Ted the usual inquisitive stare as he exchanged a few smiling words about the coming weekend and the chances of the nearby town's football team. It left Ted thinking he could already hear the sound made by a ball being kicked to the shouts of the crowd. So close, so far.

Then they came to the hospital itself, signposted in effect by some idle stretcher trolleys and a cluster of wicker laundry baskets with the prison name emblazoned on them in large black lettering, standing to one side of the entrance doors. It hadn't taken as long as Ted had been hoping in the exaggerated promise of those first steps on leaving the cell and which now quickly faded as the drab grey of the walls suddenly changed to a bold, clinical white in keeping with the sickly faint odour common to hospitals began to make itself felt. He remembered leaving but nothing of being brought there after being found unconscious in the cell; his mind turning inward as that day came back to him, it had all the similarity of a dream forgotten on waking and revisiting him during the day, the drowsy sleepiness of the one contrasting oddly with the wider consciousness of the other. He had been nearer then. But it's different here, a voice was whispering in his ear, get wise, look around, here you must first become a ghost before you die. It's in the regulations.

Appearing out of nowhere, a tall, thin man with a stethoscope dangling around his neck, passed, giving them a quick, nervous smile; he saw the back of someone in a wheelchair being pushed into a room by a nurse in a short, white coat, but couldn't tell if it was Gordon or not. Through the partly-opened door of the small ward he'd been in not so long before, he caught a glimpse of an old man with a bald head, a lifer by the look of him, sitting on a bed, and thinking this could be himself in years to come, wanted to slink away to find some, peaceful, dark corner in which to give up on the world and the future it had set aside for him.

Feeling a tug on his arm, he turned to see the officer pulling him to a stop about to knock on one of the unmarked doors they were about to pass, the words, "Here we are, then," coinciding with the rap he made on the door with the back of his hand, before pushing it open and putting his head through the opening, saying, "I've got Green here, sir, is it okay to send him in?"

"Yes, by all means," Ted heard the reply filter out from somewhere inside the room. "Been expecting him."

"In you go, I'll be outside," the officer remarked, drawing back, his hand still on the handle of the door, as he gave him a cautionary look, adding, "So no funny business, okay," giving

Ted a further nudge in the small of his back as he closed the door after him.

"Morning Ted," the psychiatrist said, turning away from an opened briefcase on the couch-bed with a thin sheaf of papers in his hand and moving to the desk. "How are we today? Things any better? Do sit down," and puling a chair under him motioned for Ted to do the same with an encouraging smile Ted recalled as being one of many from their previous meeting, and which now, as then, made him wonder how anyone could be so happy.

"Not really," he replied, pulling the chair under him and shaking his head in agreement with the remark.

"I take it you're off the anti-depressants?" he was asked, as the psychiatrist took a quick glance at one of the papers on his desk, before looking up again.

"Yes," Ted nodded, "they said I could become too used to them."

"How about the nightmares? Are you still having them?"

"I've always had them. They never really go away."

"How are things generally? Are you managing to fit in with the way they do things here?"

"I suppose so. You have to, don't you, there's not much choice, is there."

"I mean, you're not confined to your room all day, as in some prisons they are, of course."

"No, that's true. Not so far, anyway." He didn't add that he preferred staying in his cell, the door open, instead of going down to the recreation area with the others. It also meant there was a better chance of avoiding his things being stolen.

"Good... I'm pleased you could make it. Well, at least you look and sound a lot better than when I last saw you. Of course, there is a school of thought that says now you're here there's nothing more to be done, that this is all a waste of time and money. Lock them up and throw away the key, as it were. I expect you're familiar with such expressions. However, as a psychiatrist and someone who cares about people, or likes to think he does, I am in complete disagreement with that, my own training and experience leading me to believe that very little is as black and white as it so often seems. As I'm sure someone like yourself will understand only too well, having such a personal insight into an offence and what leads up to it, rather than as someone who can only try to see it from the outside, let's say. Which is where I come in, of course... someone there to look at things a little more closely and where possible, perhaps offer some kind of reason or explanation why such things happen as they do. Ted, today I want to ask you a few questions about your background... your past, that is. I know something about it, of course, but I'd like to learn more about it from your own experience. You don't have to tell me anything unless you want to, that goes without saying, I hope. I'm not here to make you comply with any rules of regulations, or to extract confessions from you, so to speak. That isn't my job. This is just between ourselves, between us – you and me – my own aim being to help you as much as I can, as I think I said when we last met. Now I can't be fairer than that, can I, so how does it sound to you? I mean, if you would find it embarrassing or feel you're not up to it, let me know and we can stop right here. No one will think the worst of you, believe me."

Unable to resist the friendliness and warmth being shown him, Ted found himself touched by a solicitude in direct contrast to the lack of personal regard and understanding inherent in the prison system and the attitudes and pettiness of the officers he came into daily contact with.

"Alright by me," he said, trying a faint smile of his own in further agreement to what was being asked.

"Good. That's better," came the bright reply, answering the smile with another of his own. "Now I know what I'm about to say may seem a little odd, but I want you to tell me just why you do think you're here. Can you do that for me? I mean, superficially speaking, we all know or think we know why, but how many of us really know or understand anything about the real, underlying reasons for it, apart from yourself, that is, as I said earlier. Can you help me there?"

His words, and the quiet, understanding authority invested in them give substance to the pause that followed as he waited patiently for Ted to speak.

"I don't know..." Ted shrugged, trying to collect and gather his thoughts about the inner vastness opened up by the scope of the question. "There's something wrong with me, isn't there, that's what they said..."

"Who said? Who told you that, Ted?"

"A lot of people," Ted said, pausing before he spoke and then pausing again. "It was in the newspapers." He paused once more, the words sticking as they came to grief in his throat. "They said I was a... you know... a paedophile. That's why I was attacked when I was on remand..."

"Even so," the psychiatrist replied, taking this in and nodding quietly, "tell me what *you* think, Ted. Do you think you're a paedophile, someone who goes around looking for sex with young girls?"

"No," he was answered after a short hesitation, "I don't think so. I've never abused anyone, if that's what you mean."

"Exactly!" the psychiatrist exclaimed, the word accompanied by a positive, knowing movement of the head.

"You're no more a paedophile than I am, despite all the things that have been said. To put is simply, you may *love* young girls, idealising them, let's say, but you aren't a lover of them, strange as this may seem to some people. Oh, don't get me wrong, I'm not condoning or seeking an apology for what you did anymore than I am condemning you for it. That's something that had already been done, hasn't it. You see, Ted, what we have to try and establish is why you felt attracted to young girls, or at least to this one girl, and who, because of her age, need I add, and the immaturity that goes with it, was not really in a position to reciprocate your interest in her, which in any case, as I say, does not appear to have been sexual, at least not overtly so. On the contrary, and this is why I find the situation regarding yourself to be so interesting, I think there are, perhaps, even more reasons for this emotional need you had, and which, in turn, have led to you finding yourself here."

Leaning slightly forward, he shuffled one or two of the papers on the desk, glancing at each in turn before going on.

"Looking back over the details of your life, it seems in many ways that what happened was an attempt on your own part – however unconsciously – to re-create and re-live the past, one that was so abruptly ended for you when, first your mother, and then your sister, died so tragically. Caught up in that past which happened when you were so young, it seems almost like a lapse of memory, does it not, to have done what you did that night without giving any thought or consideration to its consequences. The past you had known, or what became an enticing resemblance to it, then took the place of reality, as it had been threatening to do for some time, over many years, perhaps. At least in your imagination... a fantasy you had to live out no matter what the cost might be when you finally awoke to find the dream ended and you were arrested. I would even suggest that underlying this emotional and psychological need – and I would like to stress this to be an emotional and not a sexual or physical need – is the grieving I believe you still have for your sister and for that enormous sense of loss and isolation you never really recovered from when she, too, died. As a young boy, you would have idolised her and so found in these other young girls a substitute for her, and because you had also lost your mother, you needed the affection of an older woman, such as your wife, whose name I believe is..." His voice tailing off, he put out a finger on one of the sheets of paper to indicate the name he was looking for. "Oh yes, Anna. You had loved and lost both, and from then on, alone in the world, continued to look for them in one way and another. And then..." He stopped almost as the sentence began, a sadly knowing expression briefly entering his face and words as he went on, "and then, you met this other girl... and suddenly, in that magical, irresistible moment, your sister was there with you once more, together with all the pain and anxiety that came with the fear of losing her again..." he said, his voice again dying away and then resuming, its measured, thoughtful tone emphasised by a quiet seriousness. "We call this, your reaction, I mean, psychopathic tenderness..."

Breaking off, he looked away towards some other part of the room and then idly down at the papers, as sobs began to come from the figure sitting opposite him.

"She was so beautiful, so nice... I didn't mean to... to do what I did..." Ted gasped as he made futile attempts to wipe the tears streaming from his eyes, the words coming out as punctured fragments of bitter remorse.

"I know you didn't," the psychiatrist said, compassion coming into his face and voice. "I wouldn't have expected that of you, anyway."

"I only wanted to be with her..." Ted was saying, his voice so low and faraway it was as though he was talking to himself. "I loved her... I wanted to be with her... but she wanted to go away... I tried to stop her but she..."

"Like your sister, you mean, Ted..."

Not a question requiring an answer, none was forthcoming as Ted dissolved into further tears, nodding unhappily as they fall helplessly down his cheeks.

"I'm sorry Ted, all this has obviously brought to the surface a great deal of pain." He paused, his voice softly considerate. "Do you have a handkerchief, Ted?"

Seeing Ted shake his head, he got up and going to a cupboard on the far side of the room came back with a box of tissues in his hand.

"It's a funny thing, isn't it," he said, a good-natured irony entering his voice, "but in every male prison I go to there's always a shortage of handkerchiefs. Now I wonder why that is."

CHAPTER 18

He had always been self-consciously ashamed of the lies he told Anna, and by this he didn't so much mean those told directly to her face but the ones done behind her back, so to speak, and which he was forced to keep to himself. After their initial meeting and the emotional and physical excitement it entailed, he had begun to find making love to her so unfulfilling that rather than bring them closer together as intimacy should, it became instrumental in driving him further away even though he did his best to hide it. It became something he had tried to deal with in a number of surreptitious ways in order to keep the relationship and marriage intact. Outside of the bedroom – he hated the phrase love nest and grimaced upon hearing it – it hadn't been too difficult to cover up his disaffection, but when day gave way to night and expectations arose, his delaying actions could only be partly successful as there was only a certain amount of time needed to be fiddling with the light switches and cleaning your teeth, as you went on playing for time in the hope that when you eventually got to the bedroom the sidelight would be out and she would be asleep or otherwise too tired. But the enormity of the complete truth came when he admitted to himself that not only wasn't she his type, whatever that was, but that she was far too old for him even if, statistically speaking, not so old herself. At forty, she had ceased to attract and interest him as Kate and Julie had, or any of the other girls he sometimes met when wandering about, telling them he was an artist or photographer and asking if he could take their "pictures". The most revealing aspects of all this, and the hardest to reconcile himself to, had been that getting married had been his idea all along, an already-hurt Anna only agreeing to it some time later. At that time he had told himself it was what he needed, a relationship and the security that went with it not long after coming out of prison and the emotional and sexual deprivation of his earlier sentence.

Of course, to some extent he had been consciously aware that it was a big step he was taking, but on leaving prison he was without family, had nowhere to go, and had been clutching at any leaf in the wind when he and Anna had met by chance in the park where both of them, without much else to do, had been feeding the ducks and swans on one of those dismal Sunday mornings the lonely and dispossessed know only too well. With his innate dislike of crowded places like pubs – the smell of beer made him feel sick – the small lake in the local park was somewhere he had always found it easy to meet and talk with passers-by walking their dogs, or just sitting in the sunshine. Even on wet and cold days there was always someone or other about, and even if there wasn't it didn't take much to get him out of the hostel once the change from prison life began to wear off. At least, inside the prison there had been others to talk to if one wanted. It hadn't been so far from the park – well, even the centre wasn't so far away in a town that size – he had met Kate four or five years earlier, another sudden, chance meeting that not so long after was to lead to his serving that first term of imprisonment. He'd been twenty when he was convicted on a charge of "taking and removing an underage girl from the custody of her parents," a description which may not have been the exact wording but which still made him smile when he thought of it and Kate, who at the time had been only six months short of her sixteenth birthday, even if she did look younger. At that trial quite a lot had been said about him remaining susceptible and overtly sensitive to the two personal losses that had taken place in the years leading up to it, and when he had been described as being "immature" and "young for his age". His mother dying when he was ten, the more frequent absences of their father had drawn him and his thirteen year-old sister, Susie, closer together: left for the most part to fend for themselves, they became quite inseparable, with Susie as the older one becoming dominant in this. After the funeral, they began staying with their grandmother at weekends, going there on a Friday night and staying until Sunday, when they returned to the house so as to be ready for school the next day. Their father had carried on working, leaving the house each morning before they, he and his sister, set off for school, while in the evenings, after a snack or a quick meal, he usually went out and came back late, generally after they had gone to bed, where alone or huddled together in his or her bed, as they had so often done when younger, they would listen and wait for him to come in before anxiously settling down to sleep. At first, she would tuck him in, as his mother had done, before going back to her own bed, but on waking up in the dark, silent house now devoid of his mother and the routine they had once had, he would more often than not find his way into hers, as, still half-asleep, he stumbled into her room and standing by her bed put out his hand to shake her shoulder, saying in a pleading voice as he tried to choke back the tears, "Please can I come in with you, Susie?" At first a little grumpy at being woken up, she would say, "Oh, alright," pulling him in beside her and placing a reassuring arm around him as she tried to make room in the single bed. He had grown to like that, being close to her when he woke up in the night to wonder why his mother had left them, crying into the pillow and hoping she would come back before giving in to the fears and doubts that sent him impulsively running into his sister's room where he felt safer and less alone, closer to the presence of the mother he went on missing. Lying there, close to her, before they finally fell asleep, and trying not to cry again, he would ask about her, when she would be coming back, and feeling her arms around him and the warmth of her breath on the back of his neck as she hugged him, would hear her say, "Mum won't be coming back, Ted, you know that, don't you. She was ill and had to go away, so she's better where she is, isn't she. Now go to sleep or you'll be tired in the morning and we'll be late for school."

After breakfast, they would walk there together, and in the afternoon when it ended, wait for each other at the gate, where on some days he would walk behind her and a group of other girls from her class, until coming to the road where they lived she would join him again, often with her just ahead of him as she was bigger and walked a little more quickly. When his mother was there, he would make for the television in the lounge until she called him for tea in the kitchen, with Susie either helping her or coming down from her room upstairs, their father coming in later. But after she died and the house on the day of the funeral was filled with people he didn't know, he stopped watching the television in the cold, empty room, not wanting to be there alone, and began to sit in the kitchen watching his sister getting the food ready and trying to help where he could when she asked him. Their father would come in, they were always pleased to see him, have something to eat while talking to them, asking them about school and what they had been doing, before going upstairs and coming down later wearing his suit or a change of clothes telling them he was ready to go out. Then saying he wouldn't be late and telling them to be good, he'd kiss Susie on the cheek, ruffle Ted's hair with a smile, the shutting of the street door after watching him leave the kitchen a further reminder that they were on their own. At such times, and being a practical girl, Susie would emulate her mother by continuing to do what she had seen her do a hundred times or more. Together they would clear up, with Ted bringing the things from the table to the sink and his sister doing the washing-up to make sure he didn't break anything. Then while she vanished into her room to do her homework, Ted went into his, trying to read when not looking out of the window, half-listening and waiting for her to reappear, at which point he would follow her downstairs to see what she was doing. "Don't forget your bath Ted. I've turned the immersion on," she would say, calling out to him if he had gone down to the kitchen before her, or if he was in the toilet. "I've left a towel out for you."

After his bath, she would have hers, before they went down to the kitchen and in their pyjamas have something to eat and drink while watching television. Once, coming out of his room, he saw her leaving the bathroom with nothing on, and her back to him, scoot hurriedly into her own room, only partly closing the door behind her; thinking nothing of it he went towards the door, but she must have heard him and with a laugh in her voice said, "Ted, you're not peeping, are you?" as she moved to close the door, pulling her dressing-gown around her in a loss of sisterly mutuality he never understood and never quite forgot. Just as he was to never forget or fully understand the day that was to inflict on him another loss when she was run over. It affected him more than anyone thought at the time, the general attitude being that as he was so young its effect on him would pass, but he still went on seeing and hearing her in the figures and voices of her friends and those other girls wearing the same navy blue uniforms as they passed him in the school corridors or clustered together like distant constellations in the recreation ground like a dream he couldn't shut out. Alone at the house, sitting on her empty bed, on more than one occasion he left his own and getting into it lay there trembling with affectionate and wishful longing. Once, seeing a girl who reminded him of Susie – she had the same blonde hair and fringe – he followed her into the local library, watching from an upstairs' window when she left to cross the road, his face pressed against the pane of glass as he went on willing her to come back.

Later on, when he was fifteen, he found a more specific way of watching and being among girls less illusory than those at school or who went on remaining strangers to him in the street, by seeing them altered into a more vibrant reality in the swimming baths. There they moved, swam about, talked and laughed, in a *private*, more immediately personal way than at school, as they left the protective secrecy of their clothes and cubicles behind to dive or jump into the water. Once immersed, you mostly saw only their heads bobbing up and down, but back in their cubicles the feet and lower part of their legs were visible, and on occasion, if you were looking from the right angle when you were in the water, a little more, as they bent or stooped to remove clothes or swimming costumes. From then on, it wasn't too much of an imaginative leap to then find an empty cubicle next to theirs – as girls had an unfailing habit of being with someone when they came to the baths – or to wait outside, and then, after they had got their tickets, follow them in, and with luck lock himself into the cubicle next to theirs, where with an insistently mounting tension listened to what they were saying or giggling about as they undressed before leaping into the pool, or sat on the side before easing themselves gingerly in, their arms and legs shimmering in the reflected light bouncing off the surface of the water. This was how, led on by such induced frustrations, he discovered the key to his problem and the impregnable, if thin, wall between him and the source of his curiosity in the form of a hand drill in his father's garden shed at the rear of the house – the type that's used to make circular holes in wood – and which on the next Saturday morning – the day when the baths were most popular, there being no school – he smuggled the drill in among his towel and swimming trunks. There, his senses themselves swimming in a sea of their own reckless trepidation, he made two small, unobtrusive holes at a certain height in the dividing wall between his cubicle and the one next to it, having first made sure it was empty. It was the culmination of a saddened fantasy come true, seeing a girl or girls approach as he watched through the windowed mesh of his own cubicle before catching devouring glimpses of them undressing and then drying off after their swim, then following them out into the cafeteria or street to see where they would go, the residual expectations aroused by these new horizons as they went on mounting within him all week, to be pleasantly relieved when on returning the next Saturday, he found the holes were still intact in various cubicles and that no diligent lifeguard or attendant had filled them in.

Around this time, between fifteen and sixteen, other revelations of an equally auspicious and far-reaching nature took place, when in his father's room he came across a magazine showing women in various stages of undress, and on some pages, without any clothes at all. Looking through it, he was both stimulated and left disappointed at not finding what he wanted in the pictures of heavily-breasted females leering nakedly out at him, and who also had hair covering those areas he was magnetically drawn towards and which had been partially observed in his adventures at the swimming baths. Leaving him thwarted and deprived, the photographs failed to impress him as the girls entering and leaving the cubicles never failed to do, even though he found some of them more intensely attractive than others. During this period of adolescent voyeurism, another incident occurred when, on focussing an eye to one of the small, discreet holes he had made some weeks before, he had seen another eye staring back at him, and had been so momentarily shaken his first impulse had been to get dressed and leave as quickly as possible, only to then find his embarrassed disquiet erased by giggles of mutual laughter coming from the other cubicle, this being an incident that so entranced and heightened his anticipation, it lured him back to the same cubicle at the same time the following week, only it never happened again and went on leaving him even more morose and disconsolate.

Conscious that these far from satisfying activities were connected to a danger he was nonetheless unable to let go of, this ever-present awareness seemed tied-in to their premature, distressing end, when the baths closed down to be eventually demolished in a regeneration scheme affecting the whole neighbourhood. This loss of weekly entertainment and the sense of betrayal it engendered, was temporarily mitigated when, on looking for an alternative venue he heard of another pool only a bus ride away, the expectations filling him falling into further, desolating ruin when he found it wasn't as amenable as the other pool had been and instead of having cubicles around the sides of the swimming area itself, they were outside it and strictly segregated as the MALE and FEMALES signs with arrows indicated. At this one, you didn't have a cubicle but put your clothes and towel into a small, metal container which you handed to an attendant in a white coat who then gave you a metal disk with a number on which you wore around your neck in return. He was so bitterly upset at finding this, he never went there again.

These then, had become preliminary steps in the progression of events leading to his arrest, when, aged twenty, he had been convicted of the charge of abduction, or more specifically, of removing an underage girl from the care and custody of her parents, a failure to prove other charges related to this incident resulting in this being the offence he was found guilty of. It was a matter, as with so much in his life, that belonged not to any premeditated or purposeful plan, but arose from within some inwardly mesmerising trance-like preoccupation and escape from an endlessly unhappy existence, out of which there now appeared before him someone to make his life finally worthwhile. A dream within a dream, as the door of the telephone box was pushed open and the sea of alarming blue took everything down into its pitiless ocean, the girl wearing the uniform of the school he had once gone to, gave him a broad fetching smile and asked if he could change a coin so she could make another call. In that one split second, embraced and imprisoned by a yearning impervious to everything but its own indefatigable outcome, he hadn't really taken any notice of the person using the phone – the glass was smeared by rain and he was, as usual, habitually locked into his own cogitations of a randomly indolent kind – when with this smile and the youthful cadences of a voice bringing back so many others that had come and gone so poignantly, he had found the change in one of his pockets as she went on apologising for keeping him waiting as she made another call. He said he didn't mind, he wasn't in a hurry, she thanked him, smiled again with eyes so blue he was sucked into them, and huddling herself back inside the kiosk to dial her number, went on enforcing that confusing loneliness about to take the ground from beneath him once she had gone. She made her call, and he made his in a pain-filled turmoil that went on hurting so far back he could hardly bring himself to dial the correct number, only to then find, among the storm of scattered wits and disorder overtaking him, her still waiting outside, arms clasped around her against the prevailing drizzle, grinning and saying in an almost apologetic manner how she had to make yet another call, to which he remarked with a desperate composure summoned up by a foretaste of the emptiness ahead, "This is like musical chairs, isn't it," and to which she replied in that unforgettable, soft-spoken winsomeness adding its own wound to the pain, "Yes, but without the chairs!"

Seeming friendly and eager to talk, he waited until she had finished, before, another future pounding in his ears, felt confident enough to ask her if she would like to join him for a coffee, she looked cold and wet, to which she readily agreed, before bounding along the wet pavement beside him as another girl had long ago, her presence inducing a vast upsurge of joyful reunion to sweep through him at having someone like her back in his life once more, as Susie and the girls in the cubicles had tentatively been.

She should have been at school, he'd known that by her uniform; she told him she hadn't felt like it, and not for the first time. There were problems at home, which is why she had been making the phone calls, to a relative, or relatives, mainly to her married sister, to try and resolve the differences between her parents and how it was affecting her. Being an only child didn't help, and hearing about the repercussions on her in the breakdown between her mother and father took him back to his own experiences, putting him in a position to offer her the sympathy and a measure of understanding she plainly needed. It wasn't long before they were holding hands across the café table, as if they had known each other for days or weeks, not just an hour or so. It was this deep and emotional responsiveness that in later years, when he came out of prison, that so attracted Anna, who until then had become convinced of male insensitivity.

On being asked what she did all day when not at school, Kate was also moving towards that moment when she, too, vaguely glimpsed another, better future opening a door for her, despite there being obstacles she wasn't quite able to see past or beyond. But here was someone who was nice and kind, friendly, who had once gone to her school, they laughed about the same teachers; who was buying her coffee and whatever she wanted, while he listened patiently to all she was saying, in itself a pleasantness she hadn't been able to indulge in for some time. "Me?" she had said, expressing surprise at the warm interest she was being shown when inside herself she didn't feel at all attractive or worthy of it. "Not very much," she started to reply as another slice of cake appeared before her. "Walk about, go to the library, amusement arcade, sometimes. If I've got the money I might go swimming or sit in the cafeteria there. You don't have to buy anything if you've had a swim, just sit waiting for your hair to dry. I love swimming, do you?"

Swimming, drowning. At this moment of renewed promise when the voices of memory were calling out louder than ever Ted didn't know if he was afloat or sinking in the sea of blue ebbing and flowing around him. All he had wanted and longed for, that bluest of blues, the heart-breaking lucidity of a sky at daybreak brought past and present together in the colour of the uniform tumultuously radiating in the shape and presence of the girl sitting opposite and holding his hand. Congested by their unfamiliarity and long abstinence, words of thankfulness and love that had sought long and vainly for their expression, poured in like an onrushing tide to fill the yearning emptiness of his heart and mind. He'd been telling himself he loved her, would do anything for her, even as she was asking for change in that first moment of truth, and in truth, long before that; for although she was a stranger and someone he'd never seen before, in emerging as she had from some deep, longed-for wishfulness that had found a home in him as a boy, she was someone who had never really gone away, but was still there, waiting at the school gate for him, the grateful tears forming at the hack of his eyes, proof of having her near him once more to dull and deaden the need that had been tormenting and persecuting him for so long.

CHAPTER 19

He found himself writing: It's that moment when they lock us in and the building sinks back into its infinite hush, that the nightmare, the story of one's life, really begins. At the trial they called my friendship with Kate, abduction, but I never thought of it in that way at the time. I wanted to be with her it's true, it was impossible not to think along those lines when everything about her was transfigured by a remembered longing I felt helpless against, it was so much part of that completeness I had come close to but had been denied me for so long. I tried telling them that, but nobody believed it then anymore than they do now, and this in itself, this misunderstanding – reminding me as it did of the dismal inertia of the empty house and the overwhelming feeling of loneliness I had to go back to – says as much as anything can about the sequence of events that have led to my being here. In any case, perhaps there isn't such an enormous or improbable gap between that day as a boy when I woke up to find Susie wouldn't be coming back, and that other equally alarming morning some twenty years later when, on picking up the paper and seeing my name mentioned, found I'd become one of those people you read about. It's impossible, anyhow, to say at what precise or actual moment someone loses their direction and begins that downhill slide ending in loss and the imprisonment that goes with it. But knowing something of the lapses involving such a fall, I continue to write and dwell on matters that have brought me face to face with myself and others like me, and of that need that leads one astray when the coming together of elements both tender and remote become part of that search I call the longest dream of all.

In the cell, a notebook and pen in his hand, Ted's mind was now almost constantly going back over the past and to those he had loved and lost: Kate, because in loving her as he did he had victimised himself by offending those who didn't understand the nature of the friendship between them. By this, he meant the police and the law itself, for taking her away even though they knew she loved him, and wanting to send her back to her parents despite her father behaving violently towards her and her mother. It upset and annoyed him, how, whenever he loved someone, this was the outcome, not only with Kate but also Julie; like his own mother and Susie, they were always going or being taken away when he was so much happier being with them. It had been the cruellest of all fate's ironies and little tricks, that he had fallen in love with someone who wasn't allowed to love him because of her age. When at the first prison, it had been sadly gratifying to find he wasn't alone in thinking as he did, far from it, and that this was a common experience shared by so many others. But this is where it stopped, this bond, if you could call it that. He was among them, but for a number of reasons, logical or not, he didn't see himself as one of them. To begin with, he didn't like "little girls", this being a subject Chapman, for one, was obsessed with, and he loathed and hated the offhand and indecent way this was talked and boasted about without any real love and affection.

Visitors were allowed once a month, but as he had none apart from the psychiatrist – you had to laugh at that! – he carried on writing, filling the pages in the notepads as he went on talking to them. The psychiatrist had said, "It will do you good," but he would have gone on doing it anyway, as he had been in the habit of doing on the outside when he had been trying to write articles and short stories. Only now, there was far more to write about as the present and future ceased to exist in the locking of the cell door and the one to the past opened as the voices of memory came flooding in among the debris of nostalgia and self-inflicted upheaval. At one point, he ran out of paper and in an idleness of despair wrote to Anna to ask if she would send him more, and unaware she had moved, spent days waiting for an answer that never came. It was then he managed to get some scraps being thrown away in the prison library. None of this had gone unnoticed by the officers "keeping an eye on him", and when he opened the door of his cell each morning one of them had got it into his head to keep saying in that twisted way they had, "How's the Bard today? Written any more plays!"

His stay in the open prison had been vastly preferable to the one where he was now; there, instead of anyone trying to kill themselves it was more a case of how and when you jumped over the fence and made a run for it, this being far easier to do than actually getting far as these places were built in the open countryside and miles from anywhere, and without outside help most who "absconded" as it was euphemistically put, were back within days, if not hours. Even so, the two systems had much in common, and then as now, both had been grim-faced and unfair in denying him any contact with Kate, even by letter. And as it had been their time together that had nourished and sustained him during his sentence, it had been this, that on release had taken him back to the district where she had been living before they went away. She would have been older then, nineteen or twenty, and he didn't know if he would recognise her or she him. Leaving the hostel room allocated to him on licence, he spent a number of days wandering about the streets, now and then catching sight of someone who may have been her, only to discover it wasn't as she drew nearer. At the same time, the picture of her he had in his head was fixed at the age she had been at the caravan in Cornwall, and not nineteen or twenty, and he was far from sure if he would have said anything to her if it had proved to be Kate. She may not even be living in the area, especially if her parents had split up as seemed most likely, and she had gone to live with her mother or even her sister. Having gone there some three or four times, he was about to give up when he saw someone he was convinced was her. Again, it was from a distance as she came out of a shop and began walking down the road ahead of him. She was taller now, her hair shorter and cut in a more adult style, as were her clothes, and being some years older, more a young woman than a girl. But in recognising once more the unmistakeable bouncy kind of walk she had, he had also become acutely aware of the disappointment edging itself into those first few moments, when, on seeing her again, the past he was always so alert to brought him up so sharply against its lost, illusory promise. This *was* Kate, but in the intervening years which he thought of as being stolen from him, she had also become someone so far removed from the girl his memories and recollections took him back to, the only thing he knew about her was that distinct, reminiscent walk.

At a discreet distance, he had begun to follow her, making a pretence of being interested in the contents of a shop window, when she stopped to look in one, the emotional change in himself making itself felt more strongly as it quickened in accordance with the unfamiliar physical changes he couldn't avoid seeing in her. And so, in not having the same life or death attraction as she once had when he couldn't take his eyes off her for a second – in becoming but another shopper in the street – those mementos of the telephone kiosk, café and days by the sea, that he had held onto for so long, now quickly began to fade and slip away as though they had never existed. She was Kate, of that he was sure, but in a truer sense, she had *been* Kate, in a time and place now gone forever. Standing in a doorway, watching as she got onto a bus, he waited until it vanished from sight among the other traffic, and it was then, feeling sorry for himself in having to turn away from the once-vibrant past into the bleak, jobless future at the hostel, that he met Anna.

www.ingramcontent.com/pod-product-compliance
Lightning Source LLC
Chambersburg PA
CBHW071414170626
46811CB00003B/1396